The Mother of All Firecrackers

Smoke was still rising from the site of the explosion when Gamma Ray Gammand and the Wonderchild came pounding up to the newly formed crater. On either side of it the twisted ends of a metal fence looked like a tangle of dead branches.

The rest of the fence, undamaged, ran on as far as they could see in either direction.

"Plasmagoric," said Wendy, peering into the blackened pit, which stretched some thirty feet from side to side. "That must have been the mother of all firecrackers."

Books by Bruce Coville

The A.I. Gang Trilogy:
  Operation Sherlock
  Robot Trouble
  Forever Begins Tomorrow

Bruce Coville's Alien Adventures:
  Aliens Ate My Homework
  I Left My Sneakers in Dimension X

Camp Haunted Hills:
  How I Survived My Summer Vacation
  Some of My Best Friends Are Monsters
  The Dinosaur That Followed Me Home

Magic Shop Books:
  Jennifer Murdley's Toad
  Jeremy Thatcher, Dragon Hatcher
  The Monster's Ring

My Teacher Is an Alien Books:
  My Teacher Is an Alien
  My Teacher Fried My Brains
  My Teacher Glows in the Dark
  My Teacher Flunked the Planet

Space Brat Books:
  Space Brat
  Space Brat 2: Blork's Evil Twin
  Space Brat 3: The Wrath of Squat

The Dragonslayers
Goblins in the Castle
Monster of the Year

Available from MINSTREL Books

BRUCE COVILLE

THE A.I. GANG

OPERATION SHERLOCK

A MINSTREL® BOOK

PUBLISHED BY POCKET BOOKS

New York London Toronto Sydney Tokyo Singapore

A Minstrel Book published by
POCKET BOOKS, a division of Simon & Schuster Inc.
1230 Avenue of the Americas, New York, NY 10020

Copyright © 1986, 1995 by Bruce Coville

ISBN: 0-671-89249-5

First Minstrel Books printing March 1995

10 9 8 7 6 5 4 3 2 1

A MINSTREL BOOK and colophon are registered trademarks of Simon & Schuster Inc.

Cover art by Broeck Steadman

Printed in the U.S.A.

For my father, who one night took me into the living room, opened the ugly brown covers of a book called *Tom Swift in the City of Gold*, and began to read. With that act he changed my life forever.

OPERATION SHERLOCK

1

Messages and Secrets

WENDY WENDELL JUMPED OVER THE PILE OF DIRTY laundry that blocked her doorway—not easy, given the size of the pile and the shortness of her legs— and tore down the hall of her California home. Skidding to a stop in front of the computer room, she groaned at the sight of the flashing red light on her parents' Synermax 2020.

When she had first heard the beeper that signaled the arrival of some E-mail, Wendy had been sure it would be for her. After all, she had been expecting to hear from that miniatures specialist in Tokyo for days now. But her own computer was sitting quiet and lifeless while the Synermax blinked merrily away.

1

With a sigh she stepped into the room and punched a command into the computer's keyboard. Her parents usually appreciated it when she printed out the mail.

To her surprise, the Synermax began to beep urgently. A message heading appeared on the console:

TO: Dr. Watson and Dr. Wendell
DATE: June 16
CLASSIFICATION: "TOP SECRET: FOR
                  YOUR EYES ONLY"
<ENTER ACCESS CODE>

Wendy shrugged. As two of the top computer scientists in the country, her parents were always getting this kind of mail. She pushed up the sleeves of her sweatshirt (actually it was her father's, all her own being, as usual, dirty) and typed in a short code.

The Synermax let out an earsplitting shriek, then fell silent. The screen went blank for a moment, then displayed a message written in large red letters:

MIND YOUR OWN BUSINESS, DAUGHTER DEAREST!

"Chips!" said Wendy. "Mom changed the code on me again."

Brushing aside a strand of her blond hair that

had escaped from its pigtail, she went to her own computer and called up a program she had written three months earlier. Then she stretched a cord between the two machines.

"Take that, silicon brain!" she said smugly.

With the program running, she headed back to her own room, figuring that in about fifteen minutes her machine—operating on a number-pattern matching approach—would find the code to unlock the secret message.

It turned out to be closer to twenty. And when the beeper finally did summon her, she was annoyed because she had gotten involved in another project. Dropping her tools, she shoved the head back on the doll she had been wiring, then scurried down the hall to fetch the printout.

Her annoyance turned to amazement as she read the message. "This," she whispered, "is absolutely plasmodic!"

A day later and three thousand miles away, Ray Gammand sat scowling in the center of his parents' elegant New York City apartment. He was perched on his basketball—his favorite position for thinking.

Only he wasn't thinking now; he was wishing.

His current wish was that adults wouldn't act so silly. This new apartment was a dream come true. But what good would it be if his parents were going to start fighting?

After a moment the Gamma Ray (as his few

close friends called him) scrambled to his feet. "Utmost importance!" he said bitterly, repeating one of the phrases he had managed to overhear during last night's argument. "Top secret!" he muttered, crossing to the window. "Chance of a lifetime!"

He pressed his face against the glass and looked glumly out over the New York skyline.

What was going on here?

He was itching to get his hands on the mysterious piece of E-mail that had arrived late yesterday afternoon. He was sure it was what had started the whole argument. But his father had stuffed the printout into his lab coat pocket, and it had remained there ever since.

It wouldn't be so bad if the fight had simply blown over, as Gammand disagreements usually did. But at breakfast this morning his father—usually cheerful to the point of being silly—had been so quiet Ray would have thought he was sick if the angry glances shooting back and forth across the table had not told him otherwise.

Now it was Ray who felt sick. Though his father had remarried two years ago, it was only in the last month or so that Ray had begun to feel comfortable, even happy, with Elinor, his new stepmother. He didn't think he could stand it if things suddenly went sour again.

And then there was this new apartment, such a step up from their last place. And—

His thoughts were interrupted by the chime that

signaled someone wanted to come up to the apartment. Ray turned to go answer it, tripped over his basketball, and tumbled to the floor. His thick glasses flew off his face and landed in the plush carpet. This was a mixed blessing: The glasses landed without breaking, but so silently he had no idea where they were.

He began groping ahead of him, moving carefully so he wouldn't accidentally crush them. Not that there weren't times that he wanted to do just that. Sometimes he thought he was the only person in the world who still wore the darn things. The eye doctor had promised that they would be able to correct his vision with laser surgery—"But not until you've finished growing."

As if he had done any of *that* in the last few years. *Short and nearsighted,* he thought disgustedly. *What a combination for someone who wants to be a basketball star!*

He continued his search in complete silence. He wanted no help, and he wanted no one to see him.

The chime sounded again. He heard his father, his voice oddly gruff, answer on the extension in the office where he and Elinor had been conferring all day. A loud buzzing sound followed, indicating that the visitor had been okayed.

Ray cursed to himself. His father and Elinor had asked not to be interrupted. They were counting on him to handle such minor annoyances, and he had goofed up—as usual.

His hands closed over something smooth and cool.

"Gotcha!" he whispered. He slipped the stems of the glasses back over his ears, and the room shimmered into focus. He headed for the door. The visitor should be on the elevator by this time. Ray began counting. Allowing for one stop on the way up and fifteen seconds to walk down the hallway, the visitor should be here just about . . .

"Now!" Ray said softly to himself as he swung open the door. He smiled. He might be clumsy, but his timing was fantastic.

The guest, about to knock, looked startled. However, he recovered quickly. "You must be Raymond," he said with a smile. "I am Dr. Hwa."

Ray looked the man over carefully and decided he liked him. Actually, he seemed slightly familiar. With a shock Ray realized it was because meeting him was a little like glancing in a mirror. Like Ray, Dr. Hwa was short and had close-cropped dark hair. However, that was where the resemblance ended. For one thing, Ray would rather die than be caught wearing the kind of carefully tailored gray silk suit Dr. Hwa had on.

For another thing, while Ray was half African, half Irish, Dr. Hwa was clearly Asian.

But the major difference, one Ray sensed immediately, was marked by the doctor's open, sunny smile and twinkling eyes. Ray himself had never been comfortable with people and found making friends a painful process. Dr. Hwa, he could tell, was just the opposite.

"Very pleased to meet you, Raymond," said the doctor, extending a carefully manicured hand.

As Ray took it he couldn't help but notice the man's ring—a thick gold band topped by an enormous ruby that seemed to glitter with a fire of its own.

He barely had a chance to tighten his grip on Hwa's hand before a shadow loomed over them. Dr. Hwa looked up and smiled. "Ah, Dr. Gammand! I hope I'm not too early?"

"Not at all," replied Ray's father cheerfully. "You're right on time."

"I try to be punctual," said Dr. Hwa to Ray, almost as if it were a secret between the two of them. He added a conspiratorial wink and then was gone, whisked away by Dr. Gammand.

Ray watched them go, amused by the contrast between his dark-skinned father, who was close to seven feet tall, and the diminutive Dr. Hwa.

Elinor Gammand joined the two men in the hallway. Then all three adults entered the soundproof computer room.

"What's going on here?" bellowed Ray, knowing that no one could hear him. "Who is this Hwa?"

The sound of the words struck him, and he began to play with them. "Who Hwa?" he repeated with a smile. "Why Hwa? Who, what, why . . . and Hwa?"

Then it hit him; he knew why the little man looked so familiar.

Gamma Ray Gammand let out a low whistle. "Holy mackerel," he whispered. "I knew Dad was good, but I didn't know he was *that* good."

He sat down on his basketball to think.

Tripton Duncan Delmar Davis scooped up the enormous orange cat that had positioned itself at the top of the stairs. "Well, Lunkhead," he said affectionately, "let's go see what the 'rents want this time."

He ambled down the curving stairway of the stately old Philadelphia home, straightening one of his father's paintings as he went. When he reached the bottom, he congratulated himself on only stumbling once. Ever since his body had suddenly shot up past six feet, his nickname—"Trip"—seemed to have taken on a new significance. It seemed like he was never sure exactly where his arms and legs were going.

Managing to step out of the path of a vacuum cleaner that was rolling itself back and forth across the expensive living room rug, he made his way to the sunroom.

His parents were sitting at the glass-topped breakfast table, drinking coffee.

"Good morning, Tripton," said his mother.

Trip winced. His full name had never been one of his favorite things. Most of his friends called him

"3-D," which annoyed his mother almost beyond endurance. His parents usually just called him Trip. His mother's use of "Tripton" meant this was going to be a heavy discussion.

"Morning," said Trip, taking his place at the table.

Lunkhead settled into his lap and began purring loudly.

For a moment no one said anything. Trip glanced at his father, then back at his mother. *What's going on here?* he wondered. Then, with a sudden flash of panic, *Are they going to tell me that they're getting a divorce?*

He beat down the thought. *That can't be it. It has to have something to do with that piece of E-mail that came for Mom the other day. The two of them have been jumpy as cats on a freeway ever since she got it.*

He looked up and gave his parents a sunny smile; he had learned long ago it was the best way to get them to talk when they were nervous about telling him something.

Elevard Crompton Davis drummed his long, paint-stained fingers on the table and smiled back at his son. His wife, Dr. Millicent Davis, sat with her hands cupped together, as if guarding some precious secret.

Since the smile didn't do the trick, Trip decided to give them a little shove. "Does this have anything to do with that Dr. Hwa who was here yesterday?" he asked innocently.

His mother looked startled. His father's dreamy eyes opened a fraction of an inch, which was *his* way of looking startled.

"Why, yes—yes, it does," stammered his mother. She looked to her husband. "Cromp?"

Mr. Davis reached out and put his hand over his wife's. He nodded to her encouragingly.

Dr. Davis took a deep breath. She glanced around, as if looking for someplace to hide. Her eyes darted over the room, from her own priceless antiques to Trip's rare tropical fish to her husband's award-winning paintings, and finally returned to her son. "Trip," she said softly. "I have to ask you to promise me something."

Trip ran a long-fingered hand through his blond hair. Now she was making *him* nervous. "Okay," he said. "Shoot."

"Silence."

He raised a pale, questioning eyebrow.

"I have to have your promise of silence."

Trip shrugged. "I can keep my mouth shut."

Dr. Davis nodded. "Good. Because you can't tell anyone about what we're going to be doing."

"What *are* we doing?" asked Trip.

"Leaving," said his father.

A chill tingled down Trip's back. "Where are we going?"

His parents locked eyes for a moment.

"We don't know yet," whispered his mother.

* * *

Rachel Phillips folded up the small instrument she had been looking through and nodded in satisfaction. It had been three weeks since the mysterious visit from Dr. Hwa had disrupted their lives so thoroughly, and at last she knew their destination. Dropping the tool into her pocket, she nudged her twin brother, Roger. The government plane they were riding in touched down with a slight bump. "The South Pacific," she said confidently. "Somewhere east of Australia."

Roger shook his head. "Can't hear you," he said, pulling a plug out of his ear. The strains of Beethoven's magnificent Ninth Symphony drifted out until he twisted the end of the plug. It fell silent, and he dropped it into his pocket. "What were you saying?"

"We're in the South Pacific," repeated Rachel as the plane taxied down the runway.

Roger shrugged. "So what's the news? I was watching the stars, too. This whole thing about landing at night so we won't know where we are seems pretty silly to me. It's *easier* to figure it out then. I'm not sure Dr. Hwa's as bright as Dad thinks he is!"

Rachel tugged at her braid, a length of hair so red it seemed to be on fire. "I think this *whole thing* is pretty fishy," she whispered.

Roger nodded, then shoved back a lock of red hair that had fallen across his own eyes. Their father often said that if nothing else had marked them as twins, the hair would have done it. People had trouble believing one such head of hair could exist. Two of them had to mean twins!

"I wish Dad wasn't being so mysterious about the whole thing. You'd think we were blabbermouths or something."

"That bothered me for a while," admitted Rachel. "But you've got to remember how everyone at Harvard was always wondering what he was going to come up with next. Like that graduate assistant who tried to make friends with us so he could get a jump on Dad's research?"

"That twit?" asked Roger with a wave of his hand. "I knew what he was up to from the beginning."

"Are you two ready?"

Their father, Dr. Anthony Phillips, had been riding a few seats ahead of them, next to Dr. Hwa. Looking up, Roger was disappointed to see that the mysterious scientist was already on his way out the door. He had wanted to corner him for a brief talk.

"As ready as we'll ever be," said Rachel glumly.

"Come on, Rach," said Dr. Phillips. "It's not the end of the world."

"No, just the end of our lives," said Roger. "Who wants to leave Cambridge for some deserted island in the South Pacific?"

Dr. Phillips's eyes widened, and he looked at his son nervously. "How did you know where we are?"

"Come on, Dad, give us *some* credit," said Rachel. "We're not your kids for nothing."

Dr. Phillips ran a hand through his thinning auburn hair. "Okay, I can guess how you figured out the location—actually I expected you to do that, if not quite this quickly. But how did you know the island is deserted?"

"Well, if it wasn't, what would be the point of keeping it secret?" asked Roger. "We'd have figured out where we were as soon as we got here anyway."

Dr. Phillips smiled. "You have a good deductive mind, son, but you're still too quick to jump to conclusions. Or sometimes you come to the right conclusion for the wrong reasons—which can be just as confusing in the long run. The point wasn't to keep you from figuring it out. It was to keep anyone *else* from knowing before we got here. Besides, the place isn't totally deserted. It used to be an Air Force base, and some of the staff has been kept on for this project."

Rachel began to giggle.

"What's so funny?" asked Dr. Phillips.

"You!" said his daughter. "One of the reasons Roger jumps to conclusions is he knows you can't resist correcting him. It's a great way to find things out."

Dr. Phillips blushed.

"There goes my secret method!" complained Roger.

"Oh, don't worry," said Rachel. "Dad can't help himself."

Anthony Phillips looked at his children and wondered, not for the first time, how he would survive the six years left until they were eighteen, and old enough to leave home. "All right, you two," he said at last. "Let's get moving."

Reaching above their heads, he hauled down the bags the two of them had brought to carry their most necessary or most beloved items. Then he grabbed his own satchel and headed for the door.

The twins followed at his heels.

"Ouch!" said a voice as Roger accidentally banged one of his cases against a seat. The voice came from inside the case.

Rachel rolled her eyes.

"Hey!" yelled the voice. "Who turned out the lights? Sombody, turn on the lights!"

"Roger," sighed Dr. Phillips, "will you please turn him off?"

Roger slapped the side of the case. "Shut up!" he said fiercely.

"Rats!" muttered the voice. "I hate it when you make me go to sleep!"

2

"Let's Blow This Popsicle Stand"

WENDY WENDELL WAS SNORING IN HER NEW BED when the pale morning light began to filter through her window. After a few moments the sunrays struck the face of a large doll dressed in diapers and bonnet that sat on the shelf opposite her bed.

Immediately the doll—known to her owner as "Baby Pee Pants"—opened her glass eyes. She crossed and uncrossed them, waited thirty seconds, then reached out to poke the doll next to her. "Hey, Blondie," she growled, in a voice that would have been better suited to a truck driver. "Time to wake up."

The second doll—a twelve-inch-tall beauty with blue eyes, waist-length blond hair, and a hot-pink bikini plastered onto a figure that would have been grotesque in real life—yawned and stretched. "Time to move it, Mr. Pumpkiss," she said wispily, nudging the teddy bear that sat on her right.

The bear's nose twitched. "Buzz off, Blondie," it snapped. Despite its words, the bear pushed itself to a standing position.

"Ready?" asked Baby Pee Pants.

The other two nodded. In unison they took a step forward, fell off the shelf, and crashed to the floor.

Still in perfect synchronization, they said a word their owner's parents would have preferred she not even know. Then they climbed to their feet and began marching across the room. "Captain Wendy," they chanted. "Calling Captain Wendy! Time to wake up, Captain Wendy!"

When they had made their way across the floor—which was like a doll-size obstacle course, given the mess that covered it—they ran into the side of Wendy's bed and fell down again. After repeating their curse word, they began trying to climb the sheets, crying, "Let us up! Let us up, Captain Wendy!"

Wendy Wendell opened her right eye and glared at the toys. "Lemme sleep."

"Let us up! Let us up!"

"Chips!" exclaimed Wendy, pushing herself to her elbows. "What did I do to deserve this?"

The toys responded, as they had been pro-grammed to: "Life is rough, Captain Wendy."

16

"And then you die," added Baby Pee Pants in her deep voice.

"Right." Rolling onto her side, Wendy pulled the sheets over her head.

"Let us up! Let us up!"

With a sigh Wendy reached down and scooped the toys onto her bed. This cued them to give her five minutes of silence.

When the time was up, the bear began to sing.

Ray Gammand dug his spoon into the strawberry jam and scooped an outrageous amount onto his English muffin. "I don't like it here," he said. "I want to go home."

"For heaven's sake, Ray, give the place a chance," replied his stepmother. "We got here after dark last night, and you haven't been outside yet this morning. How can you possibly know if you like it or not?"

Ray looked at her suspiciously. "I thought you didn't want to come here, either."

Elinor Gammand shrugged. "I didn't. But I lost that fight. Do you think I should hold a grudge about it? Your father had good reason to accept this assignment, so I figure I just have to make the best of things."

Ray scowled. "I don't want to live on an island."

"What did you think Manhattan was?" asked Mrs. Gammand, trying to hold in her smile.

17

"Well, at least it had a city on it! I hate this place."

"Then you'd better go back to your room and sit," said Mrs. Gammand, wiping a smear of jam from the side of his mouth. "There's no point in going out to explore a place you hate."

Ray sighed. No matter how hard he tried, he couldn't get Elinor to put up with his nonsense.

"I guess I can cope with it," he grumbled, shoving the last of the muffin into his mouth and grabbing his basketball. "I'll see you later."

Elinor Gammand let the smile she had been holding in blossom. It was quite dazzling, one of the things that had led to her becoming the second Mrs. Gammand. Then her face went serious again. "Don't forget what your father told you."

Ray looked puzzled. "He told me lots of things."

"Security is tight. So pay attention to the signs, and *don't* go where you shouldn't! Also, be back by eleven-thirty. Dr. Hwa has scheduled a big meeting where we'll meet the other scientists and then tour the base. For heaven's sakes, try not to be late for a change. This is an important meeting."

"Okay," said Ray. But he didn't really mean it.

By eleven-thirty he planned to be on his way back to Manhattan.

"Too much blue," said Trip Davis to his father.

Elevard Crompton Davis looked out at the early morning sea, then back to the easel he had set up

18

on the bluff above the island's eastern shore. "You're right," he said glumly.

Trip smiled.

"Look, Trip, I appreciate the advice," said Mr. Davis as he opened a tube of brown paint and smeared some onto his palette. "But the truth is, you're starting to drive me slightly mad. I know there are some other kids here. Why don't you go look for them?"

Trip's smile faded. "I don't like meeting new people."

His father paused, then wiped his brush on a rag. "I can understand that," he said at last. "But let's face it—it's new ones or no one."

"I didn't ask to come here," said Trip bitterly.

"Neither did I!" snapped his father. They looked away from each other. "Your mother . . ."

"I know," sighed Trip. "Mom-the-computer-genius has to do this." He turned away. "I'll be good," he muttered. "She'll never know how mad I am."

Turning back to the scene he was trying to paint, Mr. Davis noticed a pair of redheaded kids strolling by on the beach below. "Look, Trip," he said. "Why not see if you can get to know those two?"

No answer.

"Trip?"

No answer.

Cromp Davis turned away from his painting. His son was gone.

*   *   *

The dark-eyed woman gazed through her kitchen window, watching her son, Hap, work in the backyard. She felt another pang of the guilt that had nagged at her off and on since she and her husband had decided to stay on Anza-bora Island after most of the base personnel were shipped back to the states.

She bit her lip. The boy appeared content; tinkering with the engine of his dune buggy was one of his favorite things to do. But she was a mother, and could see beyond mere appearances. As she watched, every once in a while Hap would look up from the engine and stare out to sea. Though the salty breeze rustling through his blond hair gave him a carefree appearance, his eyes were dark and brooding.

He looks so handsome, she thought. *And so lonely. It's hard to believe he's only thirteen.* She pulled the curtain shut and went to her favorite chair. *Did we make a mistake staying on like this?*

"Where better to raise a boy than on an island?" her husband had kept asking when they were trying to decide whether to accept Dr. Hwa's offer. "The world is going crazy. This is a safer place to be."

Despite her husband's claim that he wanted to remain on Anza-bora for Hap's sake, the woman knew the real reason he wanted to stay was that he himself loved isolated places, and considered living on a nearly deserted island close to heaven.

While they had many things in common, in this matter, Hap and his father were very different. Not that Hap would ever admit it. As soon as he figured out his father wanted to stay (and it hadn't taken him long to do so), nothing could have gotten him to say he wanted to leave.

The woman smiled. Hap and his father. Her two men.

She heard a sound in the yard and returned to the window just in time to see the nearly silent dune buggy disappear over a low ridge of sand. She stood looking after Hap for some time, her fingers worrying the edge of the curtain. Maybe the new people, the scientists, would have some youngsters he could make friends with.

She certainly hoped so.

"This place is hot," said Roger Phillips as he trudged along the beach.

"And sandy," said his twin.

"And stupid!" added a third voice. It came from the leather bag the twins had been passing back and forth all morning.

Rachel grimaced. "I don't know why you wanted to bring him along. He's a pain in the neck."

"Nobody loves me!" wailed the voice.

Roger ignored it and returned to the question he and Rachel had been discussing. "So—how *are* we going to get out of here?"

"We could pretend to catch some horrible disease," suggested Rachel. Before Roger could answer, she shook her head, vetoing her own suggestion. "No, that's no good. The doctors here are bound to be better than that school nurse who used to send us home all the time. They'd figure us out in nothing flat."

"We could build a raft," suggested Roger, rubbing his thumb and forefinger together, as he did whenever he was engaged in intense thought.

"That would be dangerous," said Rachel.

"And slow," agreed Roger sadly.

"And stupid," added the voice from the bag.

Suddenly they heard a plane overhead. Struck simultaneously by a single thought, the twins began to run.

Standing on his basketball, Ray Gammand thrust his fingers through the fence and stared hungrily at the airplane sitting on the runway. The robots were almost done unloading it. Before long it would be leaving. And he *couldn't* figure out how to get on to it.

He clutched the wire in frustration. He had been stopped at the gatehouse by a robot guard demanding that he insert his ID card into a slot in its chest. Since he had no ID card, the "electronic creep" (as Ray now thought of it) had refused to let him pass.

"It's getting harder and harder for a kid to get away with anything," said Ray mournfully.

"I know just what you mean," replied a deep voice beside him.

Ray was so startled he almost fell off his basketball. Tightening his grip on the fence, he turned his gaze sideways.

Standing next to him was a tiny, snub-nosed girl dressed in a grubby sweatshirt that hung nearly to her knees. Her blond hair was gathered into two bunches that dangled at the sides of her freckled face, and her blue eyes danced with mischief.

But it was her size that immediately endeared her to Ray, who had never forgiven his body for choosing his mother's genes for height instead of his father's. He still couldn't believe the unfairness of a universe that would allow someone who loved basketball and had a father who was seven feet tall to stall out in his own growth pattern before he even reached five feet. Ray considered anyone shorter than himself a potential ally. This girl was short enough to make him want to open immediate diplomatic relations.

"So—you thinking about hopping a quick flight back home?" she asked.

Ray blushed.

"Nice cheeks," said the girl. "But dangerous. You give away too much information when you do that. Anyway, I figure the airplane's out. But maybe if we work together, we can come up with some other way to blow this popsicle stand."

"Popsicle stand?"

"Rinky-dink place; in this case a small, stupid island."

"You want to get out, too?" asked Ray.

"No, I want to stay here and rot, but I was thinking of taking a short vacation first. Why don't you get off that basketball before you fall and break your neck?"

Ray stumbled off the ball. "What's your name?" he asked.

"Wendell."

He blinked. "That's a boy's name."

"So my parents were mixed up. Actually, it's my last name. My first name is Wendy. My initials are even better. My mother and grandmother have the same name, so I'm WW III—just like the next war."

Ray frowned. Though he tried to ignore current events, the rumors of war that had been circulating for the last year had made even him nervous. "I don't think that's funny. Anyway, your mother couldn't have been named Wendy Wendell before she got married!"

"I come from a family of strong-minded women. We always keep our own name when we get married."

"Terrific," said Ray, trying to figure out if this kid was for real. "So what do people call you?"

She wrinkled her nose. "Wonderchild."

Ray was silent.

"Look, it wasn't my idea. It started with my parents. They used to call me their 'little wonderchild.' But I don't think you should hold a kid responsible for her parents' minor insanities, do you?"

Ray shook his head.

"Anyway, once I got to school, the meaning changed. My teachers couldn't believe I was for real. They used to wonder if I really *was* a child."

Ray found himself sympathizing with the teachers.

"So how about you, Ray. What do—"

Ray blinked. "I never told you my name!" he said suspiciously.

For an instant Wendy "the Wonderchild" Wendell looked confused. The look was quickly replaced by a mysterious smile. Putting her finger beside her nose, she winked and said in a deep German accent, "Ve haf our little methods, *ja?*"

Ray looked around for help.

Tripton Duncan Delmar Davis glared down at the pair of redheads blocking his path.

"This is pointless," said the girl.

"And stupid," replied Trip.

"Hey!" cried a voice from inside the leather bag the girl was carrying. "That's my line!"

"Shut up," said the girl, slapping the bag.

"Look," said the boy next to her, who was obviously her brother. "There's room for two, but not for three. It doesn't make any sense for Rachel and me to split up—"

25

"Then stay together," said Trip. "I was here first anyway."

A flicker of annoyance passed over the redhead's face. He began rubbing his thumb and forefinger together. He started to speak, but his words were drowned out by the sound of an engine starting up. The doors of the robo-truck they were standing beside slammed shut and the vehicle began to roll toward the airfield gate. Trip grabbed for it, but his fingers slid off the smooth metal.

"There!" he said bitterly. "You made me miss my best chance to get out of here."

The three youngsters watched the automatic vehicle they had been fighting over roll up to the plane. Trip imagined himself scrambling out of the truck and through the plane's cargo doors. He was sure he could have done it without getting caught. A few hours of quiet hiding, tucked behind some boxes, and he would have been out of this place.

He realized he was holding himself so tensely his shoulders were starting to ache. How he longed to go home!

Shaking his head, he turned sadly away.

The redheads started to follow him.

"It was a crazy idea anyway," said the boy to his sister. "Dad would have been worried sick."

True, thought Trip, imagining how his own parents would have reacted if he had succeeded.

"Besides, he probably would have figured out

where we had gone and been coming after us in a few hours," said the other redhead with a sigh.

Scuffing along ahead of them, Trip nodded his head. That, too, was equally true for his parents. He slowed his footsteps just a bit.

"But I did want to go home," said the boy, who was now just a few steps behind Trip.

"Where's home?" asked Trip, without looking around.

"Cambridge," said the girl. "We had a great house just a few blocks from Harvard."

Trip stopped and let the twins catch up with him. "I went there with my mom once," he said. "I liked it. I'm from Philadelphia, and . . ." He paused in midsentence. From the corner of his eye he had spotted something wrong.

In an emergency the human brain can work faster than its owner can consciously think. That's what happened to Trip at that moment. Before he could figure out what he had seen, a message from his brain made him grab each of the twins by an arm.

To their surprise, Roger and Rachel found themselves being thrust toward the ditch at the edge of the road.

"Duck!" cried the stranger.

As the three youngsters hit the dirt, a deep booming began to shake the air above them.

3

Gamma Ball

SMOKE WAS STILL RISING FROM THE SITE OF THE EX-plosion when Ray Gammand and the Wonderchild came pounding up to the newly formed crater. On either side of it the twisted ends of a metal fence looked like a tangle of dead branches.

The rest of the fence, undamaged, ran on as far as they could see in either direction.

"Plasmagoric," said Wendy, peering into the blackened pit. It stretched some thirty feet from side to side, and seemed a good fifteen feet deep. "That must have been the mother of all firecrackers!"

Glancing to their right, the Gamma Ray noticed an enormously tall blond boy, flanked by a pair of redheads who came up to about his shoulder. Behind them, even taller than the blond, loomed his own father, Dr. Hugh Gammand.

"Come on," said Ray. Grabbing Wendy by the hand, he made his way through the group of scientists and guards converging on the site of the explosion. "What happened?" he asked when he had reached his father's side.

"Something blew up."

Wendy began to laugh. Ray looked disgusted. "Thanks for the news flash, Dad."

Dr. Gammand shrugged. "Ask a stupid question . . ."

"That's what my mother always says," whispered Trip Davis to the Phillips twins.

"But what was it?" insisted Ray.

"A guardhouse," said a tall woman who had come up behind them. She had a prominent, hawklike nose. Her white lab coat set off the thick braid of glossy chestnut hair that reached nearly to her waist.

"Ah, Dr. Clark!" said Ray's father.

"Morning, Gammand," said the woman, nodding her head. "This your son? He has your eyes, if not your height."

Ray decided that he disliked Dr. Clark.

"What was it guarding?" asked the red-haired boy standing nearby.

"I beg your pardon?" said Dr. Clark.

"The guardhouse," said the boy. "What was it guarding?"

"Nothing, fortunately. Now that the military has left and the island is no longer open to visitors,

29

they've abandoned it. Originally it was built to control access to the power plant."

Dr. Clark gestured to her left. Across the crater left by the explosion the kids saw a road leading to a long, low building set at the edge of the water.

"It uses the tide," said Dr. Clark tersely. "Catches the water and turns it into electricity. Zero pollution. Great idea, if they ever get the bugs out. Sylvia built it."

"Sylvia?" asked Dr. Gammand.

"Sylvia Standish," replied Dr. Clark. "I met her yesterday. She's been here since the island was first set up as an Air Force base. She stayed on after they closed, to continue working on her project. Doesn't seem to care much for the changeover. That's her now."

Looking in the direction that Dr. Clark nodded, they saw an attractive blond woman in jeans and a blue sweater being led around the edge of the crater by a man in a military uniform. The woman was shaking, and her face was pale. She clung to the man's arm.

Four Jeeps pulled up to the crowd, and several uniformed people jumped out. Politely but firmly they began asking the onlookers to return to their workstations.

"End of the show," said Dr. Gammand. "I wonder when they'll let us know what that was all about, eh, Ray?"

There was no answer.

Dr. Gammand looked down. His son and the other youngsters were gone.

"Roger and Rachel Phillips," said the red-haired girl, completing the round of introductions. "And we feel just like the rest of you—it wasn't fair for them to drag us here against our wishes!"

The five youngsters walked in a tight group, their gloom alleviated to some extent by the excitement of the explosion.

"What do you supposed caused that blowup?" asked Trip after a while.

"Some crazy experiment, I imagine," said Rachel.

"Nah," responded Roger. "Dr. Clark said it was a guardhouse. They wouldn't be doing experiments in there."

"A gas leak?" suggested Wendy.

"Doesn't seem likely in an electrical plant," said Trip with a smile.

Wendy smacked herself in the side of the head. "Duh!" she said, making a face.

"Could it have been lightning?" asked Ray uncertainly.

"Sabotage seems more likely to me," said Trip.

The others stopped in their tracks. "Sabotage?" asked Rachel.

Trip shrugged. "This is a top-secret project, isn't it?"

"I guess so!" said Wendy. "Even *we* don't know what it's about!"

"Well, if they're keeping it this hush-hush, it stands to reason it's pretty important. And whenever someone's working on something important, there's usually someone else who doesn't want them to succeed. At least, that's the way it seems from the history I've read."

"Even so, we have no real reason to suspect sabotage," said Roger.

Trip shrugged. "I was just throwing it out as a possibility."

"How's the possibility of eating?" asked Wendy. "I'm so hungry I could eat a horseburger."

"It's only ten o'clock in the morning!" said Rachel.

"My stomach is not ruled by the clock," replied Wendy.

"Come on," said Trip. "My mother told me how to get to the base canteen. It's not far from here."

Ten minutes later the group had gathered around a table in a low, cool room. Everyone except Rachel had a soda; she was drinking coffee. The pint-size Wendy also had a huge burger and a plate of fries.

"Did you see the look on that kid's face when I ordered this?" she asked indignantly.

"That kid" was a medium-size, broad-shouldered boy of about their age. He was standing behind the counter, wiping it with a rag. Above his shirt pocket he wore a white plastic name tag that said "HAP" in big blue letters. While he worked he kept glancing toward the group at the table.

"He gives me the creeps," said Wendy.

"Gamma Ball!" cried Ray.

"Huh?"

"They've got Gamma Ball! See?" He was already on his feet and walking toward a game table set up at the back of the canteen.

"Chips!" said Wendy, grabbing her burger to follow the others. "A game freak."

"Oh, but what a game!" said Trip, pushing back his chair. "The special effects are out of this world. Come on, you can stuff your face while the rest of us play."

Ray was already feeding money into the slot when the others joined him at the table.

"Okay," said Roger, "Rachel and I will take on Trip and Ray for the championship of the island. Fair enough?"

"Fair enough," said Ray, glancing up at his towering partner. "But be warned—I'm good!"

"He's modest, too," said Wendy, wiping some ketchup off her chin. "But not so's it shows."

"Shhh!" said Trip, furrowing his brow. On the table ahead of him several three-dimensional monsters were starting to take shape. He and Ray would be controlling the orange-skinned creatures. The Phillips twins had the purples.

Ray stuck the tip of his tongue between his teeth

and began to concentrate. He loved this game! The playing table was laid out like a fantasy forest, with swamps and valleys and dangerous traps. Two teams of monsters had to battle for control of the Gamma Ball—a scarlet sphere of light that floated in the air—so they could get it back to their castle to save their wizard's life. The lifelike monsters, created by holographic projectors, made the old video games he had played when he was a kid look sick.

Each player controlled three different monsters. Several of the "dangers" were designed so that the only way the players could avoid destruction was by working together. Surviving the Pit of Doom, for example, required the strength of one of Ray's monsters and the height of one of the creatures controlled by Trip.

Rachel let out a shout. The Gamma Ball was in the air!

Ray whirled the trackballs that controlled the speed and direction of his creatures. Each monster also had a set of buttons marked Jump, Grab, Hit, Throw, and Drop. His hands fairly flew over the control panel as he guided his creatures through their maneuvers.

Beside him Trip was muttering to himself as he moved Gongor the Mighty along a tricky jungle path.

"Watch out!" cried Ray.

Too late. Gongor had fallen into the River of Light.

"One down!" crowed Rachel, just as a creature-eating vine lashed out and grabbed her own Thwom the Thwacker from behind. "Roger, help me!" she cried. Her purple monster, only three inches tall, thrashed and squealed in the grip of the plant.

Meanwhile Ray had guided Squamous the Squat, a short but powerful creature, over to help Gongor out of the river. At the same time, seeing the randomly moving Gamma Ball fly nearby, he punched both the Jump and the Grab buttons for one of his other creatures and snagged the ball in midair.

"Hey, the kid *is* good!" cried Wendy, stuffing the last of her burger into her mouth. "I'm impressed!"

Thwom the Thwacker was dead. Rachel had lost the little monster when the killer vine strangled him and threw him into the Bottomless Pit of Rangor. This was not entirely bad for Rachel; with only two monsters to control she could concentrate more fully on their individual movements. Right now she had both of them bearing down on Manzax the Mighty, Ray's creature that was holding the Gamma Ball. Grabbing some hanging vines, they swung over the river side by side.

Ray, busy with one creature trying to help Gongor and the other trying to carry the Gamma Ball into the castle, was not fast enough to catch

Rachel's moves. Suddenly her creatures jumped him and stole the Gamma Ball.

"Way to go, Sis!" exclaimed Roger, positioning his own creatures to protect her while she carried the Gamma Ball to their side of the table.

"Oh, yeah?" cried Ray. He pushed a pair of buttons and Squamous the Squat *picked up* Gongor and threw him out of the river. The little orange monster landed on his feet, made a dive, and tackled all three of Roger's creatures at once.

"Plasmagacious!" cried Wendy in amazement.

Then the machine blew up.

Or, to be more accurate, the creatures blew up. They started getting bigger and bigger—and fainter and fainter. Finally, without a sound, they faded out of sight. The jungle cries fell silent. The lights flickered and died. The Gamma Ball faded out of sight.

"Chips!" cried Wendy. "Just when it was getting exciting!"

"I wonder what happened to it," said Trip.

"Overload," said Ray. "Too many good players at once. Don't worry—I can fix it."

Much to the group's astonishment he pulled a set of miniature tools from his pocket, slithered under the table, and began singing to himself.

Fifteen minutes later delicate electronic parts were scattered across the floor next to the table.

The handsome boy who had served Wendy her hamburger was standing next to Ray's legs, tapping his own foot impatiently.

"Yeah, yeah, I'll be done in a sec," said Ray. "Any of you guys got some gum?"

"I do," said Wendy.

"Chew me up a stick, will you? Get most of the flavor out of it and then pass it on to me."

"You like gum without flavor?" asked Wendy nervously.

"It's for the machine, goofus! Just chew the gum, will you?"

"Glad to be of service," said Wendy with a shrug.

"You guys are going to be in big trouble if you screw that game up," said the broad-shouldered boy.

"Don't worry," said Wendy. "He's a genius." She paused, glanced at Ray's feet, then added, "At least, I think he is."

The boy named Hap looked more nervous than ever. "Where's that gum?"

"Cripes, gimme a minute," said Wendy. "I'm chewing as fast as I can!" A minute later she removed a gooey wad from her mouth. "Here," she said, passing it under the game table. "Don't worry about giving it back. You can keep it."

"Thanks. Now shove those parts back under here, will you?"

Trip began handing the machine's components to Ray, who hummed contentedly as he worked. Only seconds after Trip had passed in the last piece Ray shouted, "Victory!"

At the same time the game came winking and roaring back to life.

When Roger looked at the playing field, he gave a cry of surprise. "What happened to the monsters? They're all different!"

"Uh-oh," said Wendy, glancing at the young canteen attendant.

Ray slid out from under the table and flashed them a dazzling smile. "Those are the advanced level monsters. It's an option built into the machine to let it handle superior players. Most people don't even know it exists."

"How did *you* know?" asked Rachel.

"My father invented it."

"The option?" asked Trip.

Ray shook his head. "The whole game."

After a thrilling game that ended with Ray and Trip beating the Phillips twins by just a hair, the gang decided to move on.

"Keep the change," said Ray to the attendant as the group was heading out the door.

Running back a minute later to grab her leather bag, Rachel shivered at the expression she caught on the canteen worker's face.

Great, she thought. *Our first day here, and already we've made an enemy!*

*   *   *

The Phillips house was closest, so they went there.

"What was it that bothered you so much about the kid in the canteen, Wendy?" asked Roger as he dragged a two-liter bottle of soda out of the refrigerator.

Wendy shrugged. "I don't know. I guess I got the impression he thought he owned the place."

"It's to be expected," said Rachel. "We came barging in there like *we* owned the place and started taking apart an expensive machine. This kid—who's been here who knows how long—was bound to get a little uptight. Man *is* a territorial creature, after all."

"Well, I wasn't going to hurt it!" said Ray.

"But he didn't know that!"

Ray looked surprised. "I hadn't thought of that."

"Look," said Wendy, "this may seem like it's changing the subject, but that's only because it is. I want to know what you've got in that bag! You've been carrying it around like it was filled with diamonds."

Rachel smiled at Roger. "Shall we show them?"

"Why not?"

Rachel moved the leather bag from the kitchen counter to the center of the round table where the kids were sitting. As she set it down, she gave it a slight squeeze.

"Hey!" yelled a metallic voice. "Who turned out the lights?"

"Quiet," yelled Rachel fondly. "I'm going to let you out."

"Somebody loves me at last!"

"I told you to be quiet," said Rachel.

Unzipping the bag, she reached inside.

"Hey!" cried the voice. "Your hands are cold!"

Ignoring the complaint, she turned to Wendy, Ray and Trip and said: "Ladies and gentlemen, allow me to introduce—Paracelsus!"

4

"Cogito, Ergo Sum"

RAY SHIVERED. FOR AN INSTANT HE HAD THOUGHT
that the beautifully formed head Rachel pulled
from the bag was real. Then he realized it was made
of bronze. Slightly larger than an actual human head,
it had the handsome, even features of an ancient
Greek statue. Short, sculpted curls covered its skull
and chin. The only break in the smooth metallic
surface was a pair of wide, bright blue eyes that
blinked every five or six seconds, giving the automaton an amazingly lifelike appearance.

It was mounted on a two-inch-thick wooden base
that had been polished to a high gloss.

"Pleased to meet'cha," said Paracelsus.

Wendy glanced at Rachel and Roger. "Plas-
marific," she whispered.

The bronze head made a clicking noise. "I beg
your pardon?"

"I believe Wendy is impressed," said Rachel.

"Well, she should be," said Paracelsus.

Trying to stifle a laugh, Ray snorted and ended up spraying soda on the table.

"Careful!" cried Roger. "You'll gum up his circuits!"

"Help!" shrieked Paracelsus. "Spare my circuits! Spare my circuits!"

"You're all right," said Rachel reassuringly. "Now listen. I want you to meet some people."

"I like people!"

"Of course you do. Let's start with the girl on your left. Her name is Wendy."

With only a whisper of sound, the head swiveled on its base so that it was facing the Wonderchild. Once it was in position, it made a faint whirring sound.

"Hold still," said Rachel. "He's taking a picture of you for his memory bank."

"Hello, Wendy," said the head. "It's very nice to meet you."

"Now a little to your right is Ray," said Rachel.

Paracelsus turned to the right, made the whirring noise that indicated it was taking a picture, then said, "Hello, Ray. Spare my circuits, please."

"Uh, yeah. Of course."

"Now, to Ray's right is Trip."

"Have a nice time. When are you coming back?"

"Trip is his *name,*" said Rachel firmly.

"Excuse me," said Paracelsus. "Now I'm embarrassed."

"May I?" asked Trip, reaching out to pick up the head.

"Help!" cried Paracelsus. "Kidnapper! Kidnapper!"

Trip jumped back and put his hands at his side.

"Just a little security device we built in," said Roger with a chuckle. "It's okay, Paracelsus. He won't hurt you."

"Are you sure?"

"Of course," said Rachel.

"Then you may pick me up, Trip."

"The programming is fantastic," said Trip as he lifted Paracelsus from the table. "I almost hate to ask this, but have you tried the Turing test with him?"

"Beg pardon?" said Roger, Rachel, and the head in unison. The effect was eerie, and Trip set the head back on the table.

"The Turing test," said Wendy. "It's a test for A.I.—artificial intelligence."

"I remember!" said Ray. "This English scientist named Alan Turing thought it up. You separate the tester from the machine by a wall, and if the tester can't tell in six passes—six question-and-answer exchanges—whether it's a machine or a human, then it's considered artificial intelligence."

"Well, it's a little more complicated than that,"

said Trip. "For example, you're supposed to use a keyboard to get around the problems of voice quality and expressiveness. But you've got the basic idea."

"I bet Paracelsus could pass," said Wendy.

"Not likely," said Rachel. "I'll admit we did a good job with the program. In fact, I think it's one of the best Conversation Simulators in the country. We built in a lot of clever keying devices. But he's not really thinking."

"I know," said Paracelsus. "And it's too bad. Thinking is important."

Trip raised a questioning eyebrow.

"That's a good example," said Rachel. "The question of thinking comes up so often when people meet Paracelsus that we worked that response into his program. It's really simple: I feed him a few key words, he spouts back a preprogrammed response, and it sounds as if we're having a real conversation."

"But not all his responses are programmed like that," said Wendy. "They can't be!"

"No, they're not," admitted Roger. "We used a lot of the repetition techniques that were pioneered way back with the first ELIZA program. Then we built in a random factor, and something else we invented ourselves that we call the 'chatter factor.' But an awful lot of what he says is a programmed response to direct stimulus. For example, if you turn him on when it's dark, he says, 'Who turned out the lights?' "

"But that's true for humans, too," said Ray. "A lot of what we say is automatic."

"True. But *we* can think of new things."

"I think that's the center of the whole question of artificial intelligence," said Ray. "Does intelligence mean creativity?"

"I always thought the real heart of the problem was awareness," said Trip. "My mother's been working on this for a long time, and—"

"Your mother's been working on this?" interrupted Roger. "So has our father."

"And mine," said Ray.

"And both my parents," said Wendy.

A moment of silence descended upon the table. It was broken by Paracelsus, who said, "Well, isn't this *nice*. I do like a party."

"Shut up," said Rachel. She looked at the others. "Are you thinking what I'm thinking?"

"It depends," said Wendy. "But I bet I can guess what you're thinking. Do any of you know why we're here?"

"Philosophers have wondered about that for centuries," said Paracelsus.

"Not for certain," said Roger, ignoring the automaton's chatter. "All we knew when we came was that it was a top-secret government project. But the picture is starting to come into focus."

"It's not a government project," said Wendy.

The others stared at her.

"How do you know that?" asked Trip.

"I read my parents' mail. I know—it's a bad habit. But they shouldn't make it so easy."

"Easy?" exclaimed Ray. "Didn't everything about this project come in coded Top Secret?"

"You let that stop you?" asked Wendy. She sounded astonished.

The others looked confused. "Top Secret messages are electronically scrambled," said Trip.

"Oh, boy, have I got a program for you guys!" said Wendy, shaking her head. "I'll let you have it cheap, too."

"Is that how you knew my name?" asked Ray, remembering their first conversation.

"Sure. I tapped a few files to find out who was going to be here. Anyway, let me fill in a couple of details for you. First off, the name of this sand pile is Anza-bora Island."

"We figured that out from the coordinates," said Rachel.

"Yeah, well that's effective, but slow," said Wendy. "Now, let me finish. This used to be an Air Force base. But since they started putting so much military hardware in space the government has been cutting back on manned air bases planetside. This one was scheduled to be closed completely until the Feds agreed to let Dr. Hwa use it as his base of operations."

46

"So this is a civilian project with government backing?" asked Trip.

"Exactly. Now, this guy Hwa has been out rounding up the top computer scientists in the country, including our parents, for some mysterious mega project."

"I can tell you a little about Hwa," said Ray. "He's the number-one brain in industry when it comes to artificial intelligence. My father had some papers Dr. Hwa wrote, and he kept shaking his head and talking about how brilliant the guy was."

"There you go," said Wendy. "Dr. Hwa has dragged us all here so our parents can help put together some ultrasophisticated artificial intelligence program. The big question is—*exactly what is it?*"

"I think I know," said Trip.

The others looked at him.

"It's what I was starting to talk about before. The day after my mother got the message from Dr. Hwa, she went out and got a plaque. It's hanging over her terminal now. It says, '*Cogito, ergo sum.*'"

"You just lost me," said Wendy.

"It's Latin," said Roger. "But it was written by a French philosopher named Descartes. It's heavy stuff. He was trying to figure out the world, and he decided that before you could know anything else, you first had to decide if you existed yourself."

"Well, that's obvious," said Ray.

"Nothing is obvious to a philosopher," replied

47

Roger. "Anyway, *Cogito, ergo sum* was the key to his later stuff. It means, 'I think, therefore I am.' "

"So?" said Wendy.

"Don't you see?" cried Trip. "They've brought our parents here to make the *ultimate* machine. Not just a machine that can talk, or solve problems, or other tricks like that. They're going to try to make a machine that can think. More than that, they're going to try to make a machine that *knows* it thinks. A self-aware computer. A computer that can say 'Cogito, ergo sum,' and mean it! They're not just after artificial intelligence. *They want to bring it to life!*"

5

Security Measures

"THIS COULD BE THE BIGGEST THING SINCE THE Manhattan Project!" said Roger, sounding both excited and a little frightened.

"The what?" asked Ray.

Rachel had long ago gotten used to the fact that most kids her age had almost no sense of history. Biting back a sigh, she said, " 'The Manhattan Project' was the code name for the program that created the first atomic bomb."

Trip looked surprised. "I can see why this would be big. But *that* big?"

"Absolutely," said Rachel. "We're talking about a new form of intelligent life."

Wendy's eyes were bulging. "And if it could actually integrate all the data it had access to . . ." She trailed off as the possibilities overwhelmed her.

"The Breakthrough Point," murmured Roger. "Questions, *big* questions, answered at a rate—"

He was interrupted by a shriek from Paracelsus. "Time to go! Time to go! Dr. Hwa is waiting!"

The sound was so startling it caused Ray to jump and let out a little scream. "What was that all about?" he asked angrily.

Roger was laughing too hard to speak, so Rachel had to answer. "Sometimes we use Paracelsus as a kind of combination talking memo pad and alarm system. We had set him to remind us that we're supposed to go to—"

"The big meeting!" finished Ray, a look of panic in his eyes. "Oh, man—my stepmother is going to skin me alive! See you guys later!"

With that, he bolted out the door.

Trip and Wendy were close behind him.

The Phillips twins made it to the meeting exactly on time. Ray and his stepmother arrived only about five minutes behind them—largely because Mrs. Gammand had been standing at the front of the house ready to go when Ray ran up.

Dr. Hwa himself was waiting at the door. Apparently unruffled by the delay in the schedule, he greeted them with a gentle smile as they entered.

The dark-haired woman standing next to him, however, seemed very disturbed indeed. Her jaw was clenched so tightly the muscles in her cheek were jumping, and she was tapping her foot in a kind of deadly rhythm that indicated major trouble for anyone who crossed her. Indeed, properly focused the glare she gave Ray and his stepmother as they came in might well have stopped a clock—or a charging elephant, for that matter. It was a powerful look coming from a woman who was only an inch or two taller than the tiny Dr. Hwa.

Ray saw a cluster of scientists milling about a table covered with trays of miniature sandwiches. Though the scientists were all dressed in identical white lab coats, he had no trouble spotting the towering figure of his father near the center of the group.

Wendy, traveling solo, appeared a few minutes after the Gammands. Like Ray and his stepmother, she was subjected to an angry glare from Dr. Hwa's assistant. Unlike the Gammands, Wendy glared back.

The woman's most powerful look of contempt was reserved for Trip and his father, who came in last of all. They were last because Trip's father had strolled into their new home several minutes *after* Trip, looking for lunch and completely unaware that they were supposed to be anywhere else.

Trip had had a mixed reaction to his father's late arrival. It was nice, because it took him off the hook. But he found it a little disturbing to be reminded that he was more responsible than his dad. His mother's reaction on spotting them only made matters worse. She patted her blond hair, folded her arms over her chest, and arched an eyebrow at her husband and son. The icy look left no question that they were in big trouble. Trip sighed. Being sufficiently more responsible than his father to get home ahead of him wasn't good enough. He probably should have gone out to look for him.

Standing beside Dr. Davis was the hawk-nosed woman with the long braid they had met earlier that morning. *Dr. Clark,* thought Trip, digging into his memory banks.

On the other side of Dr. Clark stood a short, bald man with huge hands. A piece of shiny metal extended from the breast pocket of his lab coat, but Trip couldn't make out what it was.

Going by the lab coats, there were eleven scientists in all; twelve, if you counted Dr. Hwa. Trip glanced around. Aside from the other kids, he could see five nonscientists. Two were short, dark-haired women: Dr. Hwa's assistant, and the woman who had come in with the Gamma Ray—probably his mother. Then there were three men: his own father, rumpled yet somehow still elegant; a beefy-looking man of medium height who was wearing a military uniform; and a muscular man dressed in a tie and sports coat and looking none too happy about it.

Dr. Hwa's assistant moved to a lectern at the side

of the room. "Attention. Your attention, please!" She had a voice like a bell—loud and clear, but also musical—and a lovely Irish lilt to her speech.

The room fell silent.

"I'm glad you could all make it today." The tone of her voice made it clear she was longing to add the word *finally,* and Trip had the feeling that if Dr. Hwa hadn't been standing next to her she would have launched into a lecture on promptness as a social virtue. As it was, she simply said, "This is the first chance we have had to get you all together, and Dr. Hwa would like to say a few words."

Accompanied by a smattering of applause, Dr. Hwa walked to the lectern. As his assistant stepped down and Dr. Hwa took her place, Trip realized that they were both so short that they must have positioned something behind the lectern to stand on. Otherwise they would have disappeared when they stepped behind it!

Dr. Hwa held up his hands to silence the applause. "Thank you," he said. His voice was gentle but firm. "Welcome to Project Alpha. I am glad you are all here." His ruby ring flashed as he gripped the sides of the lectern. Leaning forward, he said intently, "More glad than you can possibly imagine."

"Oxford," whispered Roger, sidling up to Trip. "With a trace of California."

Trip raised a questioning eyebrow.

"His *accent!*" hissed Roger.

Trip nodded and wondered how Roger could possibly have figured that out. Sometimes it frustrated him how much there was to know. He felt good about the progress he was making in his studies of lasers, information transmission, and the history of art. But there was so much *else* to learn!

Dr. Hwa was still speaking. "First, I would like to apologize for this morning's excitement. Security is looking into it, but we are quite sure that it was an industrial accident having nothing to do with our work."

I'm not so sure about that, thought Trip.

"Next I would like to apologize to the young people for the swiftness and secrecy they have had to endure in coming here. One secret that I can now unveil is your location. Let me welcome you to the South Pacific—specifically, to Anza-bora Island."

A look of satisfaction passed among the five youngsters. They had pegged that one right!

"Unfortunately," continued Dr. Hwa, "most of the rest of our secrets must remain just that. We are embarking upon a project of the utmost importance. Many forces would like to have the information we will create—information that could be used in many ways, some of them good, some unbelievably destructive. So if our security measures sometimes seem harsh, I hope you will understand, and forgive us. I do not like secrecy and hiding myself.

54

But as director of this project, I am responsible for all information that leaves this base."

He looked around. "It's a responsibility I take very seriously. For that reason, we have taken serious measures. As many of you know, unlike most computers, ours is not connected to any other machines. For the duration of our project we will live without the 'Net. Moreover, we have created an electronic shield that makes it impossible to transmit information to or from this island by any but two frequencies—both of which will be constantly monitored."

Dr. Hwa smiled gently. "This is not to be taken as a sign of mistrust in any of you, of course. It is simply a sign of how important we feel the project is—how important, and how potentially interesting to outside forces.

"But let us talk of more pleasant things. Because of the significance of our work, the government has agreed to let us use the former Anza-bora Air Base as our headquarters. We could hardly ask for a more perfect spot. Not only is it isolated and secure, but much of the technical equipment we need is already in place, including a superb mainframe computer that we can adapt to our purposes.

"Even better, at least for some of you, is the fact that this gives us a very pleasant place to live—a place where families can be together, and where there are many opportunities to enjoy yourselves when not working."

Dr. Hwa sought out the youngsters and favored each of them with a smile. "From personal experience, painful experience, I know that it is not easy to leave your home. I hope that when you have begun to explore the possibilities of our island, you will feel it was worth it. The Air Force left us a great deal of equipment—including sailboats, diving gear, and even dune buggies—that will be available to you . . . depending, of course, on your passing certain safety tests and receiving permission from your parents." He paused, then with a twinkle in his eye, added, "We have also arranged for each of you to have a computer terminal in your own room."

The kids looked at each other and shrugged. They had all had computers of their own for years.

"These terminals will be linked to the island's mainframe," continued Hwa. "The meaning of this should be clear: Each of you will have constant and instant access to what will soon be the most powerful and sophisticated computer in the world. Of course, a great deal of *our* programming will be classified. But for the most part you can use the computer as you please."

The diminutive scientist laughed out loud at the look of astonished pleasure that appeared on the youngsters' faces.

"Now," he said, "I think a few introductions are in order. We are a small community, and we will be working in close proximity for some time. Of

course, many of you have already met at confer-
ences or know each other through your work. And
those of you who arrived early, like Dr. Clark and
Dr. Fontana, have had a chance to meet many of
the others. Even so, I should feel remiss if I did
not formally introduce you all."

Except for Rachel, who had studied several
memory-training techniques and could plug names
into her head quickly, there were just too many
new people for the kids to learn all at once. They
paid particular attention as each others' parents
were introduced, of course. But there were seventeen adults in all—the twelve scientists plus Ray's
mother, Trip's father, Dr. Hwa's assistant, and the
two other men. So the names and faces inevitably
become a blur to everyone save Rachel. With her
help, the others were able to sort out the crowd
later—though it took some time before they were
always sure they were matching the right name to
the right face.

In addition to their parents there was:

Dr. Celia Clark, whom they had met earlier that
morning; tall and hawk-nosed, she was distin-
guished by her long chestnut braid. . . .

Dr. Leonard Weiskopf, the funny little bald man
with the huge hands and a shiny metal tube sticking
out of his pocket. . . .

Dr. Marion Fontana, a short, pipe-smoking
woman who radiated strength and confidence. . . .

Dr. Stanley Remov, a serious looking older man whose face had more freckles per square inch than any they had ever seen. . . .

Dr. Armand Mercury, who matched the planet that was his namesake by being the smallest (and roundest) in the group. . . .

And last but not least, Dr. Bai' Ling, whose striking beauty Ray would later describe as "indescribable!"

Besides the scientists there were three other staff people at the meeting. One was the formidable Bridget McGrory, Dr. Hwa's secretary/aide—she of the deadly eyes and the laughing voice. The second was Sergeant Artemus P. Brody, who was in charge of security for the project. The third—the muscular man in the sports coat—was Henry Swenson, head of maintenance for the facility.

Of the three, only Brody spoke, making a presentation that was so astonishingly dull Wendy nearly fell asleep on her feet even though it only lasted ten minutes. The one interesting item she gathered from Brody's comments was the surprising (to her, at least) statement that with maintenance, support and security staff, the total island population was close to 120—down from the nearly fifteen hundred that had been here when the base was at full strength, but still more than she had expected.

"Now for our tour of Anza-bora!" exclaimed Dr. Hwa when Brody was finally finished. He sounded relieved. Wendy guessed it was because most of the group was still awake.

Rachel Phillips found herself wedged between her father and Dr. Weiskopf in the backseat of a Jeep driven by Bridget McGrory. While they were waiting to start, the little scientist winked at her. Then he extracted the metal tube Rachel had noticed earlier from his pocket.

Rachel smiled. She had been speculating about what the tube was, and had finally decided it must be some sophisticated technical measuring device.

Her guess had been wrong. It was a pennywhistle.

"May I play you a tune?" asked Dr. Weiskopf. A sea breeze rustled through the fringe of graying hair that made a half circle around his mostly bald head.

"My brother's the classical music lover," said Rachel. "I prefer robot rock."

A wistful look crossed Dr. Weiskopf's face. With a shrug he said, "Perhaps some other time."

"On the other hand," said Rachel as he began tucking the whistle back into his pocket, "being on an island like this puts me in the mood for a sea song."

Dr. Weiskopf beamed as he whipped the whistle out of his pocket and raised it to his lips.

Rachel's father smiled at her gratefully.

Though she was skeptical that the old man's

sausagelike fingers could manipulate the whistle at all, Rachel's tolerance turned to pleasant surprise when Dr. Weiskopf began to play. Starting with a soft, pure trill, he coaxed more music out of the simple instrument than she would have thought possible.

The song did indeed have the sound of the sea in it, and Rachel began to feel dreamy and far away. She was actually disappointed when the Jeep lurched forward and Dr. Weiskopf put the whistle away so they could concentrate on their tour.

As the tour circled the island, the kids felt a growing sense of excitement. Anza-bora was truly beautiful. Its low southern end was blessed with spectacular beaches. Its northern tip—barely five miles away—rose to a peak that stood nearly a thousand feet above the ocean. In between were the airfield, the marina, the base housing (mostly deserted now, of course) and a wonderful forest.

Later the kids would remember many things about that afternoon: their delight as they began to sense the possibilities inherent in the island's private coves and rocky shores; the way Trip Davis's father got so excited about a view he wanted to paint that he forgot to look where he was going and fell over a small cliff; Dr. Hwa smiling with pride as he pointed out a long three-story building with an odd central dome and explained that it housed the great computer which would soon be the center of their parents' lives.

But most of all they would remember finding the first of the clues that would eventually convince them one of the adults they had just met was a dangerous traitor.

6

Bugged!

IT WAS RAY WHO FOUND IT. THE GANG HAD RE-
turned to the canteen after the official tour to compare notes (and to try another round of the new,
improved Gamma Ball). Ray was rummaging through
his pockets for coins when he pulled out a small metal
square with several wires sticking out of it.

"Hmmm. I forgot about this," he said, just before
he tossed it onto the small mountain of stuff he had
already piled on the table.

"What is it?" asked Wendy, extracting the square
from the stack of paper clips, transistors, rubber
bands, and marbles.

Ray looked up from his rummaging. "What's
what? Oh, that. It's a current detector my father
and I were working on." He made a face. "I've got
to give up fishing," he said, dropping a dead worm
onto the table.

"How does it work?" asked Wendy, ignoring Rachel's squeal of disgust. "The current detector, not the dead worm."

"Got it!" cried Ray, pulling a crumpled dollar bill from his pocket. "I knew I had one in there."

"Ray!" snapped Wendy. "Forget about the money and answer me!"

The blond boy who had cooked the Wonderchild's burger that morning appeared at the table with several bottles of soda and a cup of black coffee. Setting the coffee in front of Rachel, he looked at Wendy and said, "Patience is a virtue."

"So is minding your own business! Not to mention answering questions," she added, returning her attention to Ray.

"Wendy!" hissed Rachel. "That wasn't very nice." She glanced over at the counter. The dark-eyed boy had returned to his workstation. But he was staring at them in a way that made her nervous.

"Okay, okay," said Ray, taking the current detector from Wendy. "There's a microbattery here, see? Now, these wires set up a small field that can be interrupted by any electrical activity in the area. That trips the beeper. Here, I'll turn it on."

He fumbled with the device for a moment. "Darn lint," he muttered to no one in particular. "Always gumming things up. Ah, there we go. . . ."

He looked up at the others. "Of course, there's not really much point in turning it on," he said. "It only has a range of a couple of feet, and—"

He was interrupted by a high, urgent beeping.

"That's funny," he said, furrowing his brow. "Is one of you wearing an electric watch?"

Of course, none of them was. Their watches were all powered by heat transferred from their skin.

"I wonder what it is?" said Ray, slowing moving the device around the table.

"Probably a short circuit," said Trip.

Ray snorted.

The beep was getting louder.

"Hey, Rachel, it's you!" said Wendy. "Maybe you're really a robot!"

"Yuk, yuk, I'm dying from laughter," said Rachel. "Get that thing away from me, Ray. I don't like it."

Ray's eyes lit up. "Would you prefer this?" he asked, reaching out and plucking a small chip of metal from the underside of her collar.

Rachel looked shocked. "What is it?"

"I'm not sure," said Ray. "But my guess is that you've been bugged."

Less than a mile from the canteen the gang's words were being picked up by a small but sophisticated receiver. The person hunched next to it was frowning. Already unhappy at the turn the conversation had taken, the listener tensed when Ray Gammand said "... my guess is that you've been bugged."

Instantly a black-gloved fist came crashing down

on the receiver. The little device shattered into a thousand pieces—triggering a signal that simultaneously destroyed the transmitter being held by Ray Gammand.

The code name of this secret listener was Black Glove. It was a name known only to the handful of people in the world who were even aware of the agent's existence.

The spy looked down at the remnants of the receiver and made a sound of disgust. With the discovery of the transmitter so carefully placed on Rachel Phillips's collar, the device had instantly become worthless. That was why it had to be smashed. Black Glove had no tolerance for useless things.

Moreover, the spy did not underestimate enemies. It seemed unlikely, *but not unthinkable,* for one of those kids to have some device tucked away in his or her pocket that would have let them trace the bug's line of transmission.

A device that would, in effect, have led them straight to this secret room.

Of course, they could never get into it.

But why take unnecessary chances? Planting the bug had been risky enough. Not that they would ever guess whose hand had slipped it onto the girl's collar. But even so . . .

Muttering softly, Black Glove swept the pieces of the receiver off the table and tossed them into a nearby disintegrator, where a bank of laser beams destroyed them.

Taking a deep breath, the spy eliminated any remaining anger just as efficiently.

Anger was a waste of time.

And it was one of the basic rules of espionage that there was *always* more than one way to skin a cat. . . .

With a cry of pain the Gamma Ray dropped the device he had picked from Rachel's collar. It made a brief sizzling noise, then vanished in a puff of smoke, leaving behind nothing but an acrid smell.

The five young people stared at one another in shock. The moment of silence was followed by a small uproar as each of them began to talk at once.

"All right!" yelled Roger. "Can it!"

The group fell silent. Knowing the moment wouldn't last, Roger began speaking immediately. "To begin with," he said softly, "let's get out of here and see if we can find some safe place to talk. If there was a microphone on Rachel, there could be more anywhere: tables, chairs, walls . . ."

"Us," added Wendy.

"Exactly," said Roger. "So no more talking until Ray has made a complete sweep with that little circuit detector of his."

They left the canteen as a group, ignoring the strange look that the young attendant gave them as they went.

Because they didn't know the island well yet, it took them some time to find a place where they felt secure. Finally they settled on a rocky patch of land that thrust a little way into the ocean. Before they continued their discussion, Ray took out his current detector and swept it over each of them. He found no more bugs. Rachel had been the only one "infected."

"Things are different on an island," said Wendy, looking out across the water. Of the group, she had spent the most time at the beach. But in California she had had a continent behind her when she faced the ocean. Here there was only a few miles of sand and rock, and then more ocean. She stood, looked out at the water, and felt very small.

Though she hadn't expressed it in words, the others knew what she was thinking. Anza-bora Island was like a beautiful cage; a cage with lots of room and plenty to do, but with walls as real as if they had been made of brick and mortar. If they got in trouble, there was nowhere to run.

"Sit down, Wendy," said Rachel. "You're making me nervous."

"Afraid I'll fall off the island?" asked Wendy with a bitter laugh.

"I feel like we've fallen off the *world*," said Ray. "What's going on here, anyway?"

"That's what we came out here to talk about," said Trip. "But to tell you the truth, I haven't the slightest idea."

"Well, let's start at the beginning," said Roger.

"The first thing we need to know is who put that bug on Rachel's collar."

His twin shivered. It made her nervous just to think of some unknown hand so close to her neck.

"Maybe it was put on before you got here," suggested Ray. "Even though Dr. Hwa is trying to keep the whole thing quiet, I bet there's a lot of interest in this project. Someone might have found out you guys were coming here and figured it was easier to bug you than your father."

A ripple of relief seemed to pass over the kids. It was like the moment when some pounding noise in the background finally stops and you suddenly realize how much it had been bothering you. In the same way the moment of relaxation that followed Ray's suggestion made it clear to each of the kids how worried they really had been.

Unfortunately, the moment was short-lived.

"It's a good idea, Ray," said Rachel, brushing back a strand of flame-colored hair that the ocean breeze had misplaced. "But it doesn't hold up. I was wearing this blouse last night. I spilled coffee on it before I went to bed, and this morning when I got up I threw it in the cleaner/dryer. No way that transmitter would have survived a trip through the wash cycle."

"Chips!" said Wendy. She turned around and looked out to sea again. "I want to go home."

"Don't we all!" said Trip. "But there's no point

in going on about it. We're stuck here, so we might as well make the best of it."

"What makes you so perky?" asked Wendy. She began pacing back and forth. "Did you take sunshine pills this morning?"

"All right, all right," said Roger. "Let's not debate philosophy. The question is: When did the bug get on Rachel's collar?"

"And who put it there?" added Trip.

"Well, look," said Rachel. "I put on the blouse just before Roger and I left the house to head for the meeting. Since we didn't meet anyone along the way . . ."

"It had to be someone at the meeting," finished Trip. "And assuming it wasn't one of us . . ."

"Then it had to be one of the adults," concluded Ray.

"Is it possible someone snuck into your house and planted the bug on your blouse while you were out this morning?" asked Wendy.

"Not likely. I've learned to safeguard my room because of certain pranksters in my family"—at this Roger looked at the sky and whistled tunelessly—"so I'm pretty sure I would have known it if anyone had been in my room."

"We have to consider even the slightest possibility," said Trip.

"Let's say for now it was someone at the meeting," put in Ray. "Who was close enough to do it, Rachel?"

The redhead paused for a moment. "Oh, it could have been anyone," she said unhappily. "I think each of the adults made it a point to greet me. Of course . . ." She shook her head. "No, it couldn't be him."

"Who?" cried several voices in unison.

"Dr. Weiskopf. He sat next to me in the Jeep when we took the tour. He would have had lots of time, and I would never had noticed it when we were jouncing around. But he's such a sweet little man I can't believe it was him."

"Attila the Hun's mother probably thought he was a cutie," said Wendy.

"I have to agree with the twerp here," said Trip, glancing down at Wendy. "For the moment, Dr. Weiskopf is our number one suspect."

"But the truth is, it could have been any of the adults at that meeting," said Ray.

He didn't go on to say that this meant the list of suspects included their parents.

He didn't need to.

They were all thinking it anyway.

7

Brainstorm

WENDY WOKE THE NEXT MORNING WHEN MR. PUMP-kiss climbed onto her head and began singing a mournful song about its long-lost love.

"All right, all right," grumbled the Wonderchild. "You stop singing and I'll stop snoring. Okay?"

"Of course, Captain Wendy," said the bear. Then, as it had been programmed to do, it resumed the song.

"Chips!" exclaimed Wendy. Snatching the bear from her head, she pushed in its nose.

It stopped singing.

"Why I put up with my own inventions, I'll never know," she grumbled, climbing out of bed and stumbling through the laundry scattered across her floor. To her surprise, the message light on her computer terminal was blinking.

"Awfully early for a message," she muttered to

herself. Tossing a stack of mismatched socks off her chair, she sat down at the keyboard and typed in her personal code. Despite the fact that she had been awake for only a few minutes—she usually required at least an hour to start feeling human—Wendy smiled as she did this. Having her terminal connected to the superpowerful mainframe was one of the best things about this island. Of course there was a lot on the big computer she couldn't tap into. At least, not yet. . . .

A beep from the computer interrupted her thoughts as a message flashed on the screen:

Wendy:
    Meet me at the canteen. Pronto!
                    —Rachel

"That's all?" said the Wonderchild. "Meet me at the canteen? Who does she think she is? The President?"

Despite her resentment at the tone of the message, Wendy ran a brush through her hair and bound it into pigtails. Then she began rummaging through her clothes. Finding nothing clean (she hadn't washed anything before she packed), she dashed into her parents' room and snatched a sweatshirt from her father's dresser.

Three minutes later she was heading for the canteen.

*   *   *

Clutching his basketball, the Gamma Ray trotted along the base's main road until he came to the crater left by the previous day's explosion. The air still held a touch of early-morning briskness, and beads of dew glittered on the grass. Early as it was, he was still worried that he might be late. So he sighed with relief when he saw that Trip had not yet arrived. The older boy's computer message had sounded so urgent Ray had been afraid he would be waiting impatiently.

I wonder why Trip wanted to meet here, anyway? he thought. Then, answering his own question: *Maybe he has some new idea about what caused the explosion that he wants to check out!*

Ray gazed into the crater and wondered, as he had several times in the last twenty-four hours, just what *had* caused the blast that destroyed the guard shack. Certainly he hadn't gotten any useful information from his parents, who had assured him it was simply an accident and if it was anything else Sergeant Brody and his men would see to it. His father in particular seemed very impressed by the security measures Dr. Hwa had arranged for the base.

Bouncing his ball as he walked, Ray paced back and forth at the edge of the blast site. Brody's men had constructed a temporary road around the hole and repaired the fence. A uniformed guard sat in a chair, leaning against a post and reading a paperback book. He appeared casual, but the nasty-looking rifle propped at his side made it clear he meant business.

"Well, young man, you look lost in space. What's on your mind?"

Ray glanced up and felt his mind go blank at the sight of the dark-haired woman in front of him. She was, to use his father's term, "a knockout." Slightly out of breath, she was jogging in place and looking more beautiful than any scientist had a right to.

Ray knew she was a scientist because she had been at the meeting yesterday. But he couldn't remember her name to save his life.

Pretty women always confused him that way.

She laughed—a light, silver ripple of sound that made him think of bells. His brain began to make connections. Bells ringing . . . belling . . . Bai' Ling!

"Just thinking, Dr. Ling," he said with relief. He wished she would stop bouncing. Her jet-black hair, tied in a ponytail, was swishing across her shoulders in a way that he found very distracting.

"Dangerous habit," she said, giving him a wink. "Thinking, I mean. Makes you unpopular in the real world. Of course, it's considered more acceptable for boys than for girls. Even so, if you want to have a lot of friends—stick to basketball."

"I'm a little short for it," said Ray bitterly.

"Horsefeathers! If you want to do it, do it! If you can't do everything, do what you can!" She stopped jogging and looked into the crater. "I wonder what caused that explosion." She glanced at Ray and winked again. "Dr. Fontana thinks we have a traitor in our midst. Me, I think someone was making bootleg firecrackers." She started to bounce again. "Well, I have to go. I want to make it all the way around the island this morning."

Ray watched wistfully as Dr. Ling jogged into the distance, her ponytail bouncing behind her.

"That," said a voice at his shoulder, "is one unforgivably beautiful scientist."

Ray turned to his side. "Roger! Did Trip ask you to meet him here, too?"

"Sure did. Only it seems you and I are more punctual than our friend from Philadelphia."

"Not much," said Trip, who had walked up behind them while they were staring after Dr. Ling. "Sorry if I'm a little late. What was it you wanted to see me about?"

Ray and Roger exchanged a puzzled glance.

"We didn't want to see you," said Roger. "You asked to see us!"

"Let me get this straight," said Wendy, wiping her ketchupy fingers on her father's sweatshirt. "You're here because you got a message from *me?*"

"That's right," said Rachel. She took a sip of her coffee. "And I most emphatically did not send *you* a message." She winced as she watched Wendy take a bite of burger, make a face, and then remove the top of the bun to pour a second round of ketchup over the pile of pickles and onions that already completely hid the meat.

"Well, this is more fun than a malfunctioning circuit," said Wendy. "Looks to me like one of us is losing her marbles. My grandfather always said it would happen. He didn't approve of women thinking too much."

She glanced over at the counter where the boy named Hap was whistling quietly as he stacked doughnuts in a plexiglass container. A little roborunner tottled up and down the counter, brushing away crumbs and wiping up spills. "What's he so happy about?" she snarled.

"Wendy!"

"Sorry. I guess this place is getting on my nerves. First they pluck us out of our homes and drag us off to this barfacious island. Then less than twelve hours after we get here, someone blows up a guard shack, which everyone is trying to pretend is a perfectly normal accident, though if it was I'll eat an organically grown booger while standing on my head. Next we find that microphone on your collar, which was probably placed there by one of the seventeen most important grown-ups on this dump—only we can't prove anything, because it self-destructs the minute we discover it. To top it all off, you sent me a message and I sent you a message, except neither of us sent anyone a message.

I could have more fun being flea inspector at a dog show!"

She took a huge bite of her burger and began chewing ferociously. Before she could swallow, the door to the canteen swung open and the three boys came stalking in. "Okay," said Roger, crossing to the girls. "Which one of you was it?"

"Huh?" said Wendy.

"By that," said Rachel, "she means 'which one of who was what?' "

"Come on, sis, don't play dumb. It doesn't suit you. Which one of you is playing games with the computer system? I suppose the two of you have been having a real laugh fest here while we were off at your phony emergency meeting!"

"Sit down, twin," said Rachel. "I've got something to tell you."

Roger looked at the expression on his sister's face, then nodded to his companions. Grabbing chairs, they joined the girls at the table.

Wendy and Rachel quickly filled the boys in on the messages they had received that morning. Before they could finish, everyone began talking at once.

"All right!" bellowed Roger. "Shut up!"

"You say that a lot," observed Trip.

"I have to with this group. Now look, there's something weird going on here, and frankly I don't feel comfortable talking about it in the open, if you know what I mean."

He nodded toward the counter section, where Hap was filling salt shakers.

"Let's go to my house," said Wendy. "I'll cook up some burgers."

"Was it a hurricane or an earthquake?" asked Rachel. She was standing at the door to Wendy's room, surveying the mess that covered her floor.

"Neither. I'm just domestically impaired. I keep thinking I'll wake up neat someday, but it never happens."

"It's Captain Wendy!" cried the teddy bear sitting on her shelf. "Welcome home, Captain Wendy!"

"Captain Wendy!" cried the baby doll and the fashion doll that sat on either side of the bear. "Welcome home, Captain Wendy!"

The toys stood up, took a step forward, and fell off their shelf. Cursing like sailors, they got to their feet and began walking toward the girls.

"What is this?" cried Rachel, taking a nervous step backward.

"My specialty," said Wendy happily. "Microrobotics. They're not nearly as sophisticated as Paracelsus when it comes to their speech patterns, but they can walk around pretty well. The bear's name is Mr. Pumpkiss. The dolls are Blondie and Baby Pee Pants."

"Wow," said Ray, stepping up beside the girls. "That's spooky."

"They are amazing," agreed Rachel admiringly.

"I don't mean the toys," said Ray. "I mean Wendy's room. A guy could get lost just trying to walk from one side to the other."

Wendy was about to punch him when Roger yelled, "Will you three get back out here? We've got work to do!"

"Come on," said Wendy, heading for the kitchen. "I'll tell you more about their programming later."

Ray and Rachel followed her down the hall.

A few feet after them came Mr. Pumpkiss and the girls.

The idea was born, as great ideas often are, from frustration.

"I can't make head or tail of this mess," said Ray, pushing himself away from the table. He picked up Mr. Pumpkiss, who was trying to crawl into his lap. "It just doesn't add up."

"Good grief!" cried Roger. "That's it!" He looked around the table, as if expecting the others to get it as well. "We're trying to do the adding up ourselves," he said. "Don't you see how silly that is?"

The others looked back at him blankly. But Roger was on his feet now, pacing back and forth in his excitement.

"Adding up. That's the whole point of having computers: to do the adding up! They're made to handle the drudgery—sorting, storing, comparing—

79

so the human mind can be free to do more creative things—free to do the thinking!

"Now, here we sit, beating our brains out trying to sort through these clues, and what's in the next room?" He answered his own question before anyone else had a chance. "I'll tell you what's in there: a terminal linked to what may be the most powerful computer in the world! *Will* be, by the time our parents are done with it."

Ray tried to speak, but Roger cut him off.

"So with that available, why are we sitting here like a bunch of cavemen piling up stones to keep track of our sheep? We should be writing a program—a sort, store, and compare kind of thing. Let *it* handle the data while we work on the real problem."

Trip broke in. "You mean we should write a deduction program? A sort of computer detective thing? I think you're on to something."

"On to something?" cried Roger. "You bet I'm on to something!" He stopped, and a strange expression crossed his face. He looked around the table, his eyes shining. "Stand back," he said. "I think I'm about to be brilliant."

"Uh-oh," said Wendy.

Roger began pacing again, then forced himself to hold still. His fists were clenched and he was almost trembling with excitement. "Why make a drudge program?" he asked softly. "Why not go all the way?"

"Roger?" It was Rachel. Her voice held a question that was almost a warning.

"I mean it!" cried Roger. "Hwa and our parents yanked us out of our homes and dragged us to this flyspeck in the ocean so that they can work on artificial intelligence. I say, what's to stop us from designing our own A.I. program? We've got the brains. We've got the background. And we've got what no other kids have ever done more than dream of: the world's greatest computer at our fingertips!"

He looked around the table, locking his gaze with each of the others. When he spoke again his voice was husky with the thrill of his idea. "Let's see if we can beat our parents at their own game. Let's try to make a crime-solving program *that can think for itself.* I've even got a name for the project," he added with a smile. "We'll call it 'Operation Sherlock!' "

For a moment no one said a word.

Finally Wendy put down her burger, which she had been holding halfway to her lips since Roger started his speech.

"Let's do it!" she whispered.

8

Collision Course

SUDDENLY EVERYTHING WAS DIFFERENT. IT WAS AS
if, in an instant, night had turned to day, or winter
become spring. Anza-bora Island no longer seemed
like a prison. Rather it was now a giant laboratory,
where the kids could work out the kind of program
each of them had always dreamed of creating.

Unfortunately, not everyone on Anza-bora
shared this state of bliss.

While the gang was celebrating the moment of
inspiration that had led them to their new project,
three other people, each less than a mile away,
were planning things less pleasant.

One was Black Glove. Beads of perspiration
stood out on the spy's forehead as the final adjust-
ments were made.

A sigh of relief.

Success!

Before midnight tomorrow, if all went well, every keystroke the scientists on Anza-bora Island made would be electronically transmitted to G.H.O.S.T.

Black Glove smiled in anticipation. What a delicious triumph that would be!

Elsewhere on the island a lonely member of the base population was plotting the next move in a campaign designed to confuse and upset "the intruders."

Less than half a mile from him, still another person, outraged by the idea that scientists would dare try to create a machine that could think, was putting the finishing touches on a plan to destroy the great computer that was the heart of Project Alpha.

"They are presuming to look at things that man was never meant to see," read the entry this person was writing in her small, leatherbound journal. "There is a line that humans should not cross, a division between the mortal and the immortal. This wicked project, this attempt to imitate God by making life, must be stopped. If it is not, these arrogant fools may unleash upon the world a horror that can never be recalled, a machine that could control all our lives, forever."

The secret journal in which these thoughts were recorded held page after page of similar expressions of fear and anger. The woman who had written them was genuinely convinced that they were real, and important.

And, in the way of fanatics, she was willing to

destroy anything—or anyone—to stop "the wicked project."

On the morning of their third full day on Anzabora Island none of these disturbing things were known to the five young people who had christened themselves "The A.I. Gang" on the previous afternoon.

Not that they were unaware of problems on the base. But in the excitement of beginning their new project, the problems they did know of somehow seemed distant, or easily solved.

They were gathering, according to plan, at the house of Roger and Rachel Phillips. The choice of the Phillips home as headquarters for Operation Sherlock was based on three simple facts:

1. Trip and Ray each had one parent who was at home most of the day.

2. Even though Wendy's parents were both out working on Project Alpha, no one in the group wanted to face the prospect of trying to find a path across the Wonderchild's room.

3. By the process of elimination, that left Roger and Rachel's home as the only one that was both empty and livable.

At a little after nine the first member of the gang knocked at the door.

Roger, still in his own room, buzzed him in.

"Good morning, Trip," said Paracelsus. The bronze head was sitting on the coffee table in the living room. "How are you today?"

"Just fine," said Trip. Then, without thinking, he added, "How about you?"

"Oh, I can't complain. I'm programmed not to."

Trip looked at the head. He knew many of the programming tricks that Roger and Rachel (whom he had begun to refer to as R-Squared whenever he thought of them together) had used to create the impression of intelligence in Paracelsus. Even so, he found it somewhat eerie to talk to the thing. It was so much like having a real conversation that it was hard not to think of the head as a living person.

At that moment Roger came rushing into the living room. "You're not going to believe this!" he said excitedly.

"Another mysterious message?" asked Trip, somewhat confused.

"No, but a fairly urgent one. If we get our butts down to the motor pool *right now,* we can get some training and testing on the dune buggies. Wheels, Trip! We're gonna have wheels!"

Rachel hurried in, carrying a cup of coffee in one hand, a pair of lavender high-tops in the other. "Write a note for Ray and Wendy," she suggested, plunking down on the couch to pull on her sneakers. "They can catch up with us later."

As it turned out, the two remaining members of

the gang were on their way up the walk when Trip and the twins came hurtling out of the house. Ray and Wendy readily agreed that the prospect of getting wheels was sufficient reason to postpone starting Operation Sherlock.

Despite the fact that they were all in high spirits, Trip seemed nervous as they walked along the island's main road.

"What's bothering you, Highpockets?" asked Wendy after she had watched him slowly tear three large leaves into tiny shreds.

The tall boy grimaced. "I don't know if I'm going to be able to get my parents' permission to use the dune buggies."

"Why not?" asked Ray. "It's not like there's a lot of traffic here!"

"That's not the problem," said Trip. "They just don't like cars very much. Or any kind of personal vehicle for that matter."

"Well, I can see their point," said Rachel. "But they must be reasonable about it. I mean, you had a car back in Philadelphia, didn't you?"

Trip shook his head.

"That's not unusual," said Ray. "Lots of people in Manhattan don't own cars. It's just too much hassle in the city."

"Yeah," said Trip. "But at least most of them know *how* to drive. My father doesn't even have a license! He thinks private vehicles are immoral."

"Boy, he should talk to my parents," said Wendy.

"One of their conditions for coming here was that Dr. Hwa let them bring their Volkswagen."

"Are you serious?" asked Rachel. "You've got a car here?"

Wendy nodded. "I think they have some sort of emotional attachment to the thing."

"Well, I don't think it would do any good for Dad to talk to them," said Trip. "He'd probably just offend them by calling their car an agent of environmental destruction."

Roger gave a low whistle. "Must be rough living with an artist."

"Dad's great," said Trip defensively. "He's just a little—different. Anyway, it won't hurt for me to come along for the training. Even if I can't get permission to drive, I can probably ride around with you guys."

The motor pool was located in a long, low building at the south end of the island. Though they had expected to get their training from one of the mechanics, Henry Swenson himself greeted them at the door.

"Just in time," he said, wiping his hands on an oily rag. "Another ten minutes and I would have been gone." He examined the five youngsters with a skeptical eye. "I should probably have my head examined for doing this. But Dr. Hwa is dead set on making you kids happy. So—you get to use the dune buggies. The man moves fast when he wants something; he already has written permission from all your parents."

"All right!" cried Trip, startling Mr. Swenson with his enthusiasm.

The others smiled. They were beginning to decide that however angry they might be with Dr. Hwa for dragging them to Anza-bora, he was basically a decent guy.

"This way," said Mr. Swenson, heading toward the back of the building.

When they reached the area where the dune buggies were housed a murmur of excitement rippled through the gang. The sleek little machines were beautiful. It was obvious that they had been maintained with loving care.

"First rule," said Mr. Swenson. "They go out spotless, they come back spotless. My men don't have time to clean up after you. You'll find hoses, soap, and buckets in the storage section over there."

Rachel made a mental note of the spot.

"Now, gather round while I give you an orientation to these things."

He popped behind the wheel of the closest buggy. The kids crowded in close so they could watch as he pointed out the controls and explained their uses.

"I'm going to take you out one by one to give you some personal instruction before I let you take the wheel. You can't do much damage—we'll be riding on the beach, and there's not much there you can run into. No traffic, either. Who's first?"

"You go, Trip," said Rachel. "This is your big chance."

The gangly blond didn't have to be asked twice. Wearing a grin that threatened to become slightly wider than his face, he climbed in beside Mr. Swenson. Rachel smiled when she realized that man and boy were the same height.

"Okay," said their instructor, "the first thing you do is open the door to the outside. A few years back that was standard precaution to keep you from being poisoned by carbon monoxide fumes. That's not a problem with these electric motors, of course. But it *will* keep you from driving into the wall if you get out of control."

Flashing them a cockeyed grin, he punched a button on the dashboard that activated the automatic door opener. Above them a motor hummed into action. Straight ahead a section of wall almost twenty feet wide slid silently upward.

"Ignition!" said Mr. Swenson, turning the key he had inserted into the steering column.

The little engine purred into life. "I suppose you kids would prefer an old-fashioned gas engine," said Mr. Swenson. "Loud and smelly, but exciting. Well, this one has just as much power. It just doesn't shout about it!"

With that, he and Trip were gone.

*   *   *

By noon all five kids had had a chance to race up and down the beaches with Mr. Swenson.

"I love it!" cried Wendy, bouncing out of the buggy after her first ride. "It's better than my parents' VW. It's . . . it's . . . it's plasmagunderific!"

Had there been any doubt about the Wonderchild's enthusiasm it would have been instantly dispelled by the fact that once Mr. Swenson had declared them free to drive the beaches (they weren't to be allowed on the base roads yet) and shown them the official way to sign out a vehicle, Wendy demanded that they go back out at once and "bomb around" some more. Since the others knew she had not eaten for at least two and a half hours, they found this suggestion astonishing. But none of them mentioned it. They were too eager to do exactly as she had suggested.

By midday the gang was tearing up and down the beaches on the east side of the island, spraying sand, hopping dunes, playing tag with the ocean. Trip said twice that he thought he had died and gone to heaven.

It was Ray who finally gave in. "Look, this is wonderful and all," he said. "But I *have* to have something to eat."

"Eat!" cried Wendy. "I forgot about that! I'm so hungry I could eat a blubber burger!"

Forming a pack, they headed back toward the motor pool. Trip was in front, pushing hard, trying to see how much speed he could coax out of the little vehicle.

They were shooting down a wide stretch of beach when another dune buggy suddenly shot out from behind a clump of scrub pines and cut straight in front of them.

Several things happened at once.

Trip, yelling in fright, spun his wheel hard to the right.

The other driver swerved left.

Trip, still inexperienced at handling the buggy, went into a skid. Clutching his steering wheel in terror, he spun it first one way and then the other. The little buggy danced out of his control and went sliding back and forth across the sand.

Trip, washed with panic, felt as if his stomach were trying to climb up through his throat. At the same time he had a weird sensation of being wildly alert and terribly strong.

Wendy and Ray had been driving a little behind Trip. They had also jerked their wheels to the right when the other dune buggy appeared. Trying to avoid a collision, they went bouncing into some rough scrub where the beach ended. They jolted over thick tufts of springy grass, feeling like they had been trapped in a blender.

At the same time Roger and Rachel, in separate buggies, had gone shooting off to the left. They splashed into the surf, then spun back onto dry sand.

For a moment the beach resembled nothing so much as a bumper-car ride where it had just been announced that one of the cars was carrying nitroglycerine. Instead of trying to ram each other, the six dune buggy drivers were weaving wildly back and forth, trying desperately to avoid collisions. The shouts of joy had become cries of terror.

The driver who had cut in front of Trip was the first to get his vehicle under control. He spun his buggy in a tight circle away from the others. Riding on two wheels, he ground to a stop in a screen of sand.

Roger and Rachel halted only inches apart.

Wendy and Ray came rolling slowly back to the beach.

But Tripton Duncan Delmar Davis, confused and frightened by the near collision, hit his accelerator pedal instead of his brake, flew over a small sand dune, and disappeared from sight.

9

Hap

THE FIVE REMAINING DRIVERS SHOT OUT OF THEIR vehicles like corks from a row of champagne bottles. The sand seemed to clutch at their feet as they raced toward the dune where Trip had disappeared.

Cresting it together, they faced an awful sight.

Ahead and to the right lay Trip's dune buggy. It was on its side, two wheels spinning slowly in the air, the other two buried in sand.

"It's empty!" cried Rachel before they were even halfway there.

For an awful moment no one could spot Trip. Finally Wendy shouted, "There he is—see, under that big bush, where the beach ends and the scrub begins. He looks like he's hurt!"

Indeed, Trip's long, lean form was stretched face-down some twenty feet away from them. As the gang began running toward him, he pushed himself to his hands and knees, shook his head, and let out a low moan. Before he could move again, Ray and Roger were at his side.

"Come on," said Ray, grabbing Trip's arm. "We have to help him up."

"Are you crazy?" yelped Roger. "Trip, before you make any other moves, take a deep breath and try to see if you've broken anything."

Trip shook his head again. "Nothing's broken. Come on, help me to my feet."

Once he was standing, a babble of questions broke from the gang: "Are you all right? Do you want us to go for help? Do you think you should lie back down?"

"All right!" bellowed Roger at last. "Shut up and let him catch his breath!"

Trip gave them a weak smile. "I'm okay," he said after a moment. Looking around the group, he spotted the driver who had cut in front of him. It was Hap, the boy who worked at the canteen. "You idiot!" he snapped. "You could have killed us all!"

Hap gave Trip a cold stare. "I was following an established roadway," he said. "You're the one who was roaring down the beach like it was a drag strip."

Trip swallowed. He knew the other boy was right: He shouldn't have been going so fast—especially not on his first day of driving.

Before he could apologize, Ray leaped into the argument. "Established roadway or not, only a fool would drive out into an open space like that without looking first."

"What was I supposed to be looking for? As far as I knew I was the only one on the island driving a buggy. No one told me they were going to turn the things over to a bunch of amateurs."

"Who are you calling amateurs?" cried Wendy. She was getting wound up to say more when she realized that the boy was right. They *were* amateurs.

The Wonderchild's eyebrows worked up and down furiously as she tried to think of something to say. Rachel, afraid her friend was going to explode, decided it was time to change the subject. "If Trip is all right," she said, "we'd better take a look at his buggy."

"I'm fine," said Trip. "Just a bit wobbly. Come on, let's go see what it looks like."

To their delight, the vehicle didn't look bad. From what they could see, nothing was broken or dented.

Unfortunately, there was still part of it they couldn't see.

"I think the six of us can get it upright if we work together," said Trip. He glanced at Hap to see how he would react to this suggestion. Without saying a word the sturdy blond stationed himself at one end of the buggy, ready for action.

The others found a spot to hold.

"On a count of three," said Roger. "Ready? One
. . . two . . . three!"

The buggy rocked sideways as the group pushed
on it with all their strength. But it was not enough.
Before they could get it all the way over, their
strength gave out and they had to let it fall back.

"Again!" said Roger. "One. Two. Three.
Heave!"

They leaned into it with all their might. The vehicle tipped, tottered—then fell back on its side
again.

The third try was no better.

"All right," said Rachel, "muscles are obviously
not the solution to this. Let's try working smart
instead."

All the shades in the fanatic's quarters had been
drawn, plunging her room into nearly complete
darkness. The only light was shed by a single high-
intensity lamp that cast a near-perfect circle of
brightness into the center of a desk notable for its
odd lack of clutter.

Indeed, except for the leather-bound journal in
which the fanatic was feverishly scribbling, the desk
was completely bare. Though the afternoon was
hot, anyone reading her words would have been
chilled to the bone:

"I have discovered why the explosives went off
too early and blew up the guard shack. What a
foolish miscalculation on my part! Next time I will

not make such a mistake. How fortunate that it was only a small, experimental charge, and not the full-scale bomb I shall use when it is time to accomplish my mission."

The fanatic closed the journal. Her glittering eyes stared into the darkness. *The mission.* Soon it would be time to begin the mission, the holy mission with which nothing must interfere. For nothing could be allowed to protect the monster computer from the destruction ordained for it.

Brow covered with sweat, the fanatic opened her journal and began to write again:

"Tomorrow, if I am lucky. The day after, at the latest. Then the bomb will be placed, the count-down will begin. Then sanity will triumph and this devil's project die before it has really begun.

"And if I die in the process? Small price to save mankind from this monstrosity. In my death shall be seen the glory of the human spirit—a thing no computer could ever hope to match."

A slight smile twitched at the corner of the fanat-ic's mouth. What a glorious death that might be.

Her smile grew larger as she wondered if perhaps a death that glorious ought to be shared with every-one on Anza-bora Island.

The gang had considered—and discarded—a number of wild ideas involving hand-dug trenches, jungle vines, and jumping off rocks onto levers when Hap said, "I've got some rope in my buggy."

"Why didn't you say so before?" cried Wendy.

"No one asked me. Besides, I was enjoying your harebrained schemes. But now I'm bored with them."

His manner was cool, collected, slightly mocking. The others found it infuriating.

"If you don't mind sharing, I would appreciate it if you would let us use it," said Roger stiffly.

Hap shrugged. "Why not?"

Within ten minutes he had not only provided the rope but hooked it to strategic points on Trip's buggy. After tying it to the bumper of his own buggy, he righted Trip's vehicle with just a few gentle pulls.

He untied the rope and began coiling it. "I'm late for work," he said. "See you around." Then he tossed the rope into his buggy and shot off down the beach.

"What a creep!" said Wendy as they watched him go.

"Our behavior wasn't the greatest," replied Rachel. "And we *are* still the invaders here. Come on, let's get these things back to the motor pool and head for home."

Turning, they saw Trip sitting on the sand, staring disconsolately at the side of his buggy. "Disgrace," he murmured. "Humiliation. Pain. Degradation."

Crossing to his side, they saw a dent scooped into the side of the buggy. It looked like the inside of a huge clamshell.

"Mr. Swenson is going to kill me! I'll never be able to use one of these again."

The others looked for words of encouragement, but could find none. "You're probably right," said Ray at last.

"Thanks," muttered Trip.

"Look at it this way," said Wendy gloomily. "By the time that Hap kid gets done telling his story, *none* of us will be able to use these things again."

As it turned out, the motor pool was deserted when they got back.

"I wonder where everyone is?" said Roger, troubled by the quiet.

"Maybe they took a long lunch," said Ray.

"That, or there's some kind of meeting going on," said Wendy. "I've noticed these guys are big on meetings. Probably they're talking about security again."

"They should be," said Rachel ominously, remembering the bug that had been planted on her collar the previous day. "And so should we. We'd better stop fooling around and get busy on Operation Sherlock."

Her words only added to the general gloom that had overtaken the group. In the excitement of the morning they had put aside thoughts of the strange happenings of the day before. But everyone knew Rachel was right. It was time to get to work.

In the end they left a long note for Mr. Swenson,

apologizing over and over and promising to make up for the time and energy involved in fixing the dent by doing work for him anytime he wanted.

Huddled together, they left the building.

"You're home!" cried Paracelsus. "Let's have a party!"

The five youngsters trudging into the Phillips house were exhausted, hungry and depressed, and definitely in no mood for chatter. "Shut up, Paracelsus," said Rachel.

"Wounded!" shrieked the bronze head. "Cut to the quick! My heart is breaking!"

"Do you change his programming every day?" asked Wendy.

"Once a week," said Roger. "Come on, let's get something to eat. My belly button is kissing my backbone, and I don't even want to think about a machine right now."

"Not even Operation Sherlock?" asked Ray.

"Not even a can opener until we eat! Which means it's peanut butter sandwiches, unless some miracle has happened in the kitchen."

"No burgers?" asked Wendy wistfully.

"You start the sandwiches," said Rachel to her twin, ignoring Wendy's distress. "I want to see if there are any messages from Dad."

She disappeared into the next room. Before she had been gone ten seconds, the others heard her let out a strange moan.

10

Trespassers

"RACHEL?" CALLED ROGER. "YOU ALL RIGHT?"

"I don't know. You guys better come take a look at this. *Now!*"

The others went running to join her. She was sitting at her terminal, staring at the message that appeared in large red letters on her monitor. Though it was only seven words long, it sent a chill shivering down all their spines.

BEWARE! SOMEONE IS WATCHING YOUR EVERY MOVE.

As the letters faded, Roger turned to the others. "I think we'd better get to work on that program," he said grimly.

When Dr. Anthony Phillips arrived home that evening, he found five young people sprawled across his living room floor. Each was working sep-arately—either sketching diagrams, outlining flow-charts, or poring through one of the dozens of computer manuals that littered the floor like leaves on an autumn lawn. Yet the air of furious concen-tration filling the room seemed to bind the young-sters together.

"Hello," said Dr. Phillips, setting down his brief-case. "I'm home!"

"Good evening, sir," said Paracelsus. "I hope you had a nice day."

Everyone else was silent.

"I said, 'I'm home!' " repeated Dr. Phillips, somewhat more loudly.

Roger glanced up from the table of numbers he was consulting. "Oh, hi Dad. How are you?"

Before Dr. Phillips had a chance to answer, his son had returned his attention to what he was work-ing on.

"What is going on here?" asked the scientist, more loudly still.

The angry tone in his voice caught Rachel's at-tention. "We're writing a program," she explained.

"Ah! A program!" This was something Dr. Phil-lips understood. He often became so absorbed in his own programming that he ignored everything around him. His friends still talked about the time he had scheduled a meeting at his home and was working in the living room when the other people arrived. They had held their meeting and left without him ever realizing they were there! "And what is the purpose of this program?"

"We're trying to create an intelligent machine to solve crimes," said Roger.

Dr. Phillips nodded. Then he picked up his briefcase and left the room.

Wendy looked at Roger in astonishment. "Do you think you should have told him that?"

"I never lie to my father," replied Roger. "And he almost never pays attention to what I tell him. He won't think anything more about it."

"He should," said Paracelsus. "Thinking is important."

"So is eating," said Wendy. "And *I* think it's time to do just that. Can we get together someplace after supper?"

In a matter of minutes everyone had agreed to Trip's suggestion that they meet at seven o'clock on the same rocky point where they had gone to confer after they found the bug on Rachel's collar.

"Bye, guys," said Paracelsus as they headed out the door.

To get home, Ray and Trip had to walk past the power plant. "I'd love to get in there and look around," said Trip, peering toward the mysterious building perched on the edge of the island. "It sounds like quite a system."

"Why not?" asked Ray. "My parents aren't expecting me for a while."

"But the guard..."

"I don't see any guard."

Ray was right. Though the temporary gate was closed and locked, there was no guard in sight.

"I don't get it," said Trip. "Why guard it some of the time, but not all the time?"

"I don't think there was any guard there to begin with," said Ray. "They put one on for a while after the explosion. But remember, no one was hurt in the blast, and everyone seems to think it was just an accident. Add in the fact that the island is sealed and the only people here were hand-picked by Dr. Hwa, and probably no one sees any need to guard the place. You coming?"

Ray had turned off the main road and was heading toward the fence. Trip looked around. No one in sight. He trotted along to join his friend.

When they reached the gate Ray tried the lock. It was solid. Without a word he walked along the fence to the edge of the crater left by the explosion. With a little wriggling, he quickly worked his way under the fence and into the crater.

"This is almost too easy," said Trip when he had followed Ray's lead. "I'm getting nervous."

"Do you want to see the inside of the plant or not?"

"Yes, but—"

"Well, then, come on."

The power plant was an impressive building, low in front but rising to about three stories in back.

While the front of the building was white and windowless, the soaring back half seemed to be made primarily of glass. Mysterious shapes loomed inside, some stretching almost to the ceiling.

Most fascinating to Trip was the way the building actually thrust out over the water. "I wonder how we get in?" he said, curiosity completely overcoming caution.

"We could try the door," said Ray, strolling boldly up to the front of the building.

It was unlocked.

"Come on," he said, stepping through.

Trip hung back for a moment, looking around nervously. He had an uneasy feeling that someone was watching them.

The door opened into a small office area, containing what appeared to be a secretary's desk and two glassed-off areas for private work space. At the back of the office was another door.

"Ray!" hissed Trip as his short friend headed straight for it.

"Come on, Trip! It's not like this is a private home. We're not going to hurt anything, we just want to see how the place works. Do you see any sign that says 'Keep Out'?"

"No, but . . ."

Trip's objection went unheard. Ray had already slipped through the door. Feeling jittery, Trip sighed and followed.

He was glad he did. The inside of the plant was

spectacular. In some ways it made him think of a hospital—all white, sparkling, spotless. Huge pieces of gleaming steel and glass thrust high into the air. A control panel covered with dials and blinking lights twinkled invitingly.

Most fascinating of all was the fact that the floor disappeared two-thirds of the way across the massive space. Where the polished marble ended, the sea surged and stirred restlessly, like some hungry, waiting thing.

Trip felt himself drawn to it. He was starting across the floor for a closer look when the door they had come through slammed explosively behind them.

"Well, boys," said an unfamiliar voice. "Now that you're here, what do you think of it?"

Wendy Wendell scuffed along the road toward her new home, turning the day's events over in her mind. The strange message they had found on the computer terminal made her nervous. Who could have sent it? And *how?* To do that the unknown sender either had to know the Phillipses' secret code, or somehow have cracked the machine's safeguards.

But the people on the island who had the skills to crack that computer system—herself included— could have no conceivable reason to send them such a message.

She thought again about going to her parents, or

possibly even Dr. Hwa. But what evidence did they have? The message had vanished the moment Rachel touched the keyboard.

Wendy shook her head, causing her blond pigtails to swish over her grubby sweatshirt. If only that microphone on Rachel's collar hadn't self-destructed!

She kicked at a stone. She knew what kind of reaction they would get if they tried to tell the adults about their suspicions: the brush-off. She could imagine them shaking their heads and laughing among themselves about "those kids with their hyperactive imaginations."

They would worry for a little while that perhaps the kids were too bored, then forget the whole thing.

So there's no point in telling them, concluded Wendy. *Until we can prove something, we're on our own.*

Her thoughts were interrupted by a hearty voice exclaiming, "Well, if it isn't Little Wendy!"

Wendy felt her face flush with rage. She *hated* being called "Little Wendy." She looked up, a sharp retort on her tongue, then swallowed and stayed silent. Standing in front of her was the one person on Anza-bora Island she didn't want to make any madder than he already had a right to be: Mr. Swenson from the motor pool.

"You kids have a good time today?" the sandy-haired man asked jovially.

"Yeah," said Wendy cautiously.

What was going on here? He didn't *sound* mad.

"Well, you can tell the others that I wanted to compliment you on the way you brought back the machines. A lot of the adults who use them don't take as good care of them as you did."

Wendy banged her hand against the side of her head. She had to be hearing things!

Mr. Swenson looked at her with concern. "Are you all right?"

"Sure! Of course! I was just a little surprised. We were nervous about whether or not we had brought the machines back the way you would want them." She paused, then decided to take a gamble. "Did you get our note?"

Mr. Swenson looked puzzled. "Note?"

"Uh, it was just a little thank-you note, for taking the time with us. Probably fell off or something. Well, it was nice talking with you. I have to go."

She hurried away, her brain racing. A blind man couldn't have missed the dent they had left in Trip's dune buggy. What was going on here?

The house hadn't stood empty for that long, only since the Air Force had pulled out. Yet it had a look of hollowness about it that showed anyone who cared enough to look that there was no one living in it.

The figure walking cautiously up to the back door wanted it that way. Turning the knob carefully to avoid making any sound, he slipped in through the kitchen.

He didn't stop to look around. He had been here many times before, and already knew the way.

He knew that beyond the kitchen was a living room.

He knew, too, that on the north side of the living room was a work area where the officer who used to live here had kept a computer terminal that was linked to the island's mainframe.

Though the connection had been severed when the house was abandoned, it hadn't taken much work to reconnect it.

Pulling up a chair, the invader flipped a few switches. As the terminal whirred into life, he took out a notebook. Turning to the back of the book, he found the code he was seeking.

The computer signaled that it was ready. Entering the string of numbers that would send his words where he wanted, the intruder chuckled as he began to tap out a menacing message.

11

Power Play

Beeping softly to itself, the Phillipses' robot server rolled around the corner of the table to Roger's place. Lifting the plate, it scraped the chicken bones and other bits of food into a slot in its front. A whirring sound indicated that the scraps were being ground up; later, when the robot was done with its other work, it would compress the pulverized garbage into a small brick, which it would deodorize and deposit in the garbage can.

Next the robot grabbed Roger's silverware and dumped it through a little door in its side. The pieces landed with a clatter among the utensils it had already gathered.

"All clear!" it announced. Then it rolled back to the kitchen, washing the silverware inside itself as it traveled.

"Throckmorton has been working pretty well since we replaced that chip," said Dr. Phillips.

"It's certainly an improvement over the night he stacked the garbage and ground up the plates," said Rachel.

Dr. Phillips winced at the memory. "It wouldn't have been so bad if we hadn't had half the people I work with over for dinner that night."

The twins laughed as they recalled the confusion the malfunctioning robot had caused.

"Of course, that could hardly happen here," said Roger. "Dr. Remov would jump up and fix it on the spot."

He winked at Rachel, who settled back to see how much information her twin could pull out of their father this time.

"Now, there you go again," said Dr. Phillips. He took a sip of his coffee, which he had barely rescued from Throckmorton's cleanup mission. "I don't know where you got the idea that Dr. Remov is an expert on robotics. His specialty is code systems—both how to encode material for a computer to use, and how to create codes so that no one else can get at the stuff. He's such a nut on the subject I sometimes wonder if there isn't a secret message written in his freckles."

"It must be a relief to have someone like that on a project this important," said Roger.

"It sure is," said Dr. Phillips. "If we can actually create—"

He stopped in midsentence, put down his coffee

cup, and glared at his son. "Roger, are you trying to pump me for information?"

It would have been hard to find a baby that looked more innocent than Roger Phillips did at that instant. "I was just making conversation, Dad," he said, a wounded note in his voice.

"Well, let's converse about something else," said his father.

Rachel held her stomach and tried to keep from laughing.

"Do you always walk into a place without knocking?"

The speaker, a tall blond woman who appeared to be in her late thirties, had her arms folded over her chest. Her eyes were dark and fierce.

Trip moved a step closer to Ray. He tried to calm himself, to slow his heart, which was beating against his ribs like a parakeet trying to escape from its cage.

"We just wanted to see how this worked," said Ray.

Trip was impressed with his younger friend's apparent coolness. Why couldn't *he* be that calm?

The woman arched an eyebrow. "A little scientific curiosity?"

Suddenly Trip got angry. The tone of the question and the look on the woman's face were identical to those of a teacher who had tormented him through one long and agonizing school year because she refused to believe he could possibly be interested in the things he wanted to learn about.

"That's right," he said sharply. "That's just what it is. And you needn't act so superior. I suppose we shouldn't have come in without asking, but we certainly weren't going to hurt anything. And we thought we might learn something. It's not like there's anything outside that says this place is top secret or off limits."

The woman seemed amused. "My name is Standish," she said. "Dr. Sylvia Standish."

"We know," said Ray. "We saw you the day the guard shack blew up."

A flicker of emotion passed over the woman's face. "An unfortunate accident. I'm grateful that no one was hurt."

"Anyway, there's no one on guard now," said Trip. "So we thought it might be all right to come in."

With a heavy emphasis on the *might,* this was only a slight stretch of the truth.

"That guard shack was only used when the air base was in operation," said Dr. Standish. "We had a lot of people coming onto the island then, and the security seemed like a good idea. Once the Air Force left there was no need for a guard. A good thing, too, since it meant there was no one there when the shack blew up. The only reason we've had a guard posted out there the last few days was that some people were afraid the blast might actually have been aimed at the power plant."

She shook her head, as if the idea was too ridiculous to consider. "They pulled the guard this afternoon because Dr. Hwa finally decided that it was an accident. Which only makes sense. There's no logical reason for anyone to want to sabotage this power plant."

"Could you tell us a little about how it works?" asked Trip.

Dr. Standish smiled. Trip smiled back. He had yet to meet a scientist who didn't get friendlier when asked to explain an idea.

"The whole thing is based on very simple principles," said Dr. Standish. "The most basic one is this: Every day trillions of tons of water move across the face of the earth in response to the pull of the moon. Properly harnessed, that would be an inexhaustible source of astonishing amounts of non-polluting power. The trick, of course, is figuring out how to harness it. That's what this installation is meant to do. Here, look at this."

Dr. Standish strode past the boys to where the marble floor met the sea. Again Trip felt the almost magnetic pull of the water.

"Look down there," said Dr. Standish.

The water seemed only a few feet deep—except just in front of their feet, where a shaft plunged downward. Running down the right side of the shaft was a metal track that disappeared into the water.

"That shaft goes down about fifty feet," said Dr. Standish.

Trip and Ray squinted into the murky depths, but could not see the bottom.

"Wait here." Dr. Standish strode to the control panel and threw a large switch. A light went on deep in the water, and they could see more clearly. At the bottom of the shaft was what appeared to be some sort of box.

"I have a hundred of these shafts lined up here," she said, motioning to either side of them. "At the bottom of each shaft is a box like the one you can make out down there. Now look up." She pointed to the structures that thrust toward the ceiling. "When the tide is out, counterweights in those arms pull the boxes back to the level of the floor."

She made a gesture with her head. "Come here, I'll show you one."

She led them to a work area several feet away. "This box is up for repair," she said, gesturing to a clear cube about ten feet in height. Leaning against it was a grille made of the same clear material. The crisscrossing bars, each about as thick as a man's little finger, divided it into inch-square boxes.

"This goes across the top," said Dr. Standish, tapping the grille. "It catches large debris that might clog the drains. When the boxes are pulled to the surface, the grille automatically pops up so that a powerful spray can clean off any gunk that has accumulated on it."

"What's it made of?" asked Ray, walking around the enormous cube.

"A new form of Plexiglass. It's almost indestructible. Now, when the tide comes in, it fills this box with one thousand cubic feet of seawater."

"A little over thirty-two tons," said Trip, doing a quick calculation.

Dr. Standish looked impressed. "That weight carries the cube down the shaft. The depth of the shaft varies, according to the drilling conditions we encountered. Some of them go down a hundred feet or more."

"Let me guess," said Trip. "You've got a turbine system that the tide boxes pull against. When they're full, their weight rotates the turbines to generate electricity."

Dr. Standish nodded. "Very good."

"How do you get rid of the water?" asked Ray. "Once the tide goes out, the shafts must still be full."

"Three ways. First, there's a drainage system at the bottom of each shaft. But that can only handle some of the water. We also have a siphon system. But again, that can only handle some of the water. The rest is pumped out, which, of course, uses up some of the energy. Too much. That's the main flaw in the system right now. Once the shafts are drained, the counterweights draw the boxes back to the surface and the whole cycle starts over again. It's a nearly perfect system—a power source we can't use up and that causes absolutely no pollution."

"Awesome," said Trip. "Why aren't more of these being built?"

"Cost."

The bitter tone in Dr. Standish's voice was so harsh it made the boys catch their breath.

"Cost," she repeated. "And blindness. This installation was designed to prove the concept can work. But right now the power it generates is too expensive to make it a reasonable alternative to nuclear plants, primarily because of the drainage problem. Given this situation, does the government provide the research money needed to solve the final problems and make this clean, efficient source of unlimited power more economical? Don't be silly. It funds another computer!"

With that she turned on her heel and stalked away, leaving the boys alone at the edge of the water.

Wendy Wendell III could never figure out which was worse: when her mother didn't cook—or when she did.

"I don't want to hurt your feelings Mom," she said. "But a burger would have been just fine."

"Oh, piffle," said Wendy Wendell II. "You'd take a burger over anything—and almost anything in the shape of a burger, which will probably get you in trouble someday. It's good for you to try some other foods."

"I know," sighed the Wonderchild, gazing down at the mess on her plate. "But seaweed and tofu? I mean, it looks—"

"Wendy!" warned her father, Dr. Werner Watson, inventor of the famous Watson Double Memory System. "Not at the table!"

"That would have been good advice for this food," said Wendy under her breath.

"Captain Wendy! Captain Wendy!" cried Mr. Pumpkiss, who was waddling down the hall with Blondie and Baby Pee Pants marching along behind him. "You've got a message, Captain Wendy."

Wendy looked at her parents. "I'd better go check this out. It might be important."

Her mother shrugged. Taking that as permission, Wendy was out of her chair before either of her parents could say a word. Scooping up Pumpkiss and the girls, she shot down the hall to her room.

The message light was blinking on her computer. Wendy sat down and typed in a command, then waited expectantly, thinking perhaps it was something important from one of the gang.

The terminal whirred briefly, then red letters began to dance across the screen.

BEWARE. YOUR DOOM IS WAITING.

Wendy let out a little scream. But before her parents could make it to her room, the message had vanished.

12

Remov and Mercury

THE GANG GATHERED, ACCORDING TO PLAN, ON THE
small spit of land that thrust out into the ocean. A
stiff breeze, warm and pleasantly salty, was making
whitecaps on the water.

Trip and Ray started the meeting by thrilling the
others with the story of their escapade in the
power plant.

Next Wendy told her story.

"It was like getting a crank phone call by computer," she said, describing the ominous message
to the rest of the group. "Between that and the talk
I had with Mr. Swenson, I'm beginning to think I'm
losing my marbles."

"Which is a problem," said Ray. "Since you
didn't have that many to begin with."

"I don't get the thing with Mr. Swenson at all,"

said Trip, as Ray dodged the Wonderchild's fist. "I was sure he was gonna kill us."

"Maybe someone fixed the machine before he saw it," suggested Rachel.

"Who?" asked Wendy.

"And why?" added Roger.

"And Hwa," finished Ray, almost instinctively.

"Do you really think so?" asked Trip.

"Think what?"

"That Dr. Hwa had the machine fixed? Or maybe just told Mr. Swenson not to say anything to us about it. He does seem bound and determined to be nice to us."

"Well, he owes us for dragging us to this place," said Roger.

"Even so, that's carrying nice to the outer limits," said Wendy. "The guy is okay, I suppose. But I doubt he had anything to do with this."

"Then who did?" demanded Rachel.

"This is where I came in," said Ray.

"Well, something has got to be done," said Roger.

"Remov!" cried Rachel.

"This conversation is impossible!" shouted Ray. "What are you talking about?"

"Dr. Remov," said Rachel. "He's the island's code specialist. I think he's involved with security, too. I bet he can help us trace those messages."

"Do you think we can trust him?" asked Trip.

Roger shrugged. "Can we afford not to?"

*   *   *

"Well, to what do I owe the pleasure of this visit?" asked Dr. Remov. The freckle-faced scientist was standing at the door of his house, staring at the five youngsters with some puzzlement.

"We need to talk to you," said Roger, who had appointed himself spokesman for the group. "It's urgent."

"Well, then, come in," said Dr. Remov. He stood aside so the gang could enter. "You know my friend, Dr. Mercury, I presume?"

Dr. Armand Mercury, short and round, heaved himself to his feet and came waddling out of the living room. "Of course," he said jovially, tucking a large black pipe into his pocket. "We met at Dr. Hwa's little get-acquainted party. How good to see you all again."

"I must say," said Dr. Remov as he led the way to the living room, "I'm rather happy with the houses they've provided for us. When Dr. Hwa told me we would be living on an abandoned Air Force base, I hardly expected anything this pleasant."

"Officers," said Dr. Mercury, picking up a bowl that sat next to his chair. "They always did know how to live right. You know that, Stanley."

To the gang's astonishment, Dr. Mercury then took his pipe from his pocket, dipped it into the bowl, and began blowing bubbles.

"Lovely things, aren't they?" he asked of no one in particular. "Always was partial to 'em."

"Now," said Dr. Remov, ignoring his friend, "what brings you here?"

"We wanted to know if you could help us trace a message," said Roger. "Someone is sending threatening notes to our terminals, and we want to find out what's going on."

"Dear me," said Dr. Mercury. There was a twinkle in his voice. "You don't suppose it's G.H.O.S.T., do you, Stanley?"

The five youngsters looked at him in puzzlement. "Ghost?" asked Rachel.

"This is no joking matter, Armand," said Dr. Remov sternly. Turning to the kids, he added, "Despite Dr. Mercury's jollity, G.H.O.S.T. is a real group. The name is an acronym standing for General Headquarters for Organized Strategic Terrorism."

"Balderdash!" said Dr. Mercury, who had just produced a remarkably large bubble. "The whole idea is nonsense, no more real than Bigfoot and UFOs. The group doesn't exist, any more than their mysterious agent"—and here he wiggled his fingers and made a spooky face—"*Black Glove.*"

"I tell you, it does!" cried Remov, his face growing red. "And it's fools like you who make them so powerful, Armand. You'll sit there saying they don't exist until the day they take over the world."

"Pay no attention to Stanley," said Dr. Mercury, poking his finger through a bubble that was hovering in front of his round face. "He tends to get overexcited. It goes with the freckles."

"That," said Dr. Remov in a low but deadly voice, "is about as scientific as saying that fat people are always jolly."

"Low, Stanley," said Dr. Mercury, sounding hurt. "That was very low." Picking up his bowl of bubble water, he headed out of the room. "I'll leave you people to your own devices," he said as he disappeared into the kitchen.

Behind his freckles Dr. Remov's face was still red. "Two things," he said tersely. "One: You should know that G.H.O.S.T. *is* a real group, and their chief operative is an agent named Black Glove. Like my portly friend Dr. Mercury, many people who should know better do not believe that either the group or the spy actually exist. They claim it's all some nutball conspiracy theory. But I saw too much in my years in intelligence work— intelligence as in spies, not computers—to believe that. The group *is* real, and a grave menace to the peace of the world."

Having gotten that out of his system, Dr. Remov seemed to relax. "The second thing is, I think it highly improbable that your mysterious messages are coming from G.H.O.S.T. Though the group might be interested in this project, I can't think of why it would stoop to threatening you. More likely it's some prankster here on the island."

Dr. Remov took a sip of some heavy amber liquid. "Come here," he said. "I want to show you something."

He led the way to an adjoining room, where he turned on a computer terminal. "Watch these codes carefully," he said. "I will show them to you only once."

Fingers flying over the keyboard, Dr. Remov typed in a series of numbers. Wendy, watching Rachel watch the keyboard, was satisfied that their memory expert had recorded Dr. Remov's movements.

A map appeared on the monitor. Numerous red circles were scattered across it, some solid, some blinking.

"This shows us all the terminals on the island," said Dr. Remov. He squinted at it for a second, then said, "My goodness. Look at that!"

The gang gathered closer.

"Look at what?" asked Ray at last.

"That!" said Dr. Remov, pointing a long finger at a certain circle. "That shouldn't be there."

"How do you know that?" asked Wendy.

"Because I looked at the chart before."

"And memorized it?"

He looked pained. "Of course. And don't tell me I couldn't have done it, because just now I watched you making sure your friend memorized the code I used to pull this up. So you know it can be done, even if you can't do it yourself."

Wendy took a step back. This guy was spooky!

"Now," said Dr. Remov, "that mark is located in one of the abandoned housing units about a mile up the road. I would wager it's where your messages are coming from."

Suddenly the red circle began to blink.

"You're in luck!" cried Dr. Remov. "It looks like your mysterious messenger is at work right now!"

Halfway across the island a figure wearing black gloves slipped into the ultra-restricted basement of the computer center. The spy smiled. All the advance preparation had paid off. In fact, things were going so smoothly, the job was almost boring.

Unlocking the door of the central chamber, Black Glove entered the super-cooled room where the computer was housed. What a delight this machine was; a true monument to the mind of man! All it would take was the right scientists, the right programming—the right brains gathered in the right place—and this machine could change the world.

In fact, in all the world only one computer could match the potential power of this one. Of course, the necessary scientists could never be convinced to work on *that* machine. They would be appalled at the very idea.

But that didn't matter anymore. With this transmitter in place, their work would be *sent* to that other computer. Black Glove's smile grew broader. If the Project Alpha scientists only knew what they were really creating! It would change the world all right—but not in the way they expected.

Once at the heart of the computer, the spy made a final check of the transmitter to verify that its switches were set properly. It would have been more comfortable to do that outside the chilly chamber, but also more risky.

Everything was in order. Time to begin the final installation.

Though shivering, the agent chuckled contentedly while working. How these smug scientists would react if they knew there was an electronic spy in the very heart of their great computer; knew that soon every keystroke they made, every idea they recorded, would be sent elsewhere!

The task was nearly finished. Black Glove gave the wires a final check, then applied the carefully designed cover that would hide the transmitter from anyone doing repair work here.

That done, the spy scurried back to the door, peeled off the black gloves, stuffed them into the pocket of a white lab coat and slipped out of the refrigerated area.

Now Black Glove made no effort to stay quiet, to avoid being seen. Without the transmitter to conceal, being seen was no problem—especially if anyone who might spot you would instantly recognize your familiar face, and automatically assume that you were here for a good reason.

13

The Mad Messenger

WITH BARELY A WORD TO DR. REMOV, THE GANG went barrelling out of his house and down the road.

Despite their speed, when they arrived at the house to which their new friend had directed them, they found that whoever had been using its terminal had already fled.

Even so, it wasn't long before Dr. Remov was proven correct in his belief that the mysterious messenger had been in action again. When Trip Davis arrived home that night, he found the message light blinking on the terminal in his bedroom. Nervously he punched in the code to call up the message. The words *Someone knows what you did!* flickered onto his screen.

He was not surprised when they disappeared before he could get his parents to come in and see them.

"A stakeout," said Trip the next morning as he paced back and forth in the Phillipses' living room. "That's what we need. A stakeout."

"I'd love a steak," said Paracelsus. "If I could eat."

"I'd settle for a burger," said Wendy. "But what are you really suggesting, Trip?"

"A constant watch on that house, to see who comes and goes."

"Sounds tiring," said Rachel. "Why don't you come here for a minute?"

Leading the others into the computer room (with Trip carrying Paracelsus, who begged not to be left behind), Rachel ran her fingers over the keyboard. A few seconds later the map Dr. Remov had shown them appeared on the screen.

"You've got to teach me how to do that," said Wendy.

"It's a simple code."

"I don't mean how to call up the map. I mean how to remember things that way."

"That's a simple code, too. It's a tag system. Anyone can do it with a little training. It has more to do with practice than with intelligence."

"I'm intelligent," said Paracelsus. "Alas, it's all a fraud."

"Which one of you programs that thing?" demanded Ray.

"Why?" asked Roger.

"Because one of you has a sick sense of humor, and I want to know who it is!"

"It's a secret," said Rachel. "Now listen. As I see it, we have two choices. We can set up a stakeout at the house, which would be boring and time consuming. Or we can set up something right here so that as soon as the light for that house begins to blink, we'll hear an alarm. Then we can shoot over and try to catch our mysterious messenger in action. I figure if two of us go sign out a pair of dune buggies, we could get from here to that abandoned house in just a couple of minutes when we need to." She frowned. "That's another mystery we need to figure out."

"What?" asked Ray.

"Why we can still sign those things out after what happened yesterday," said Wendy, remembering the conversation she had had with Mr. Swenson the night before.

"Exactly," agreed Rachel. She turned back to the terminal. "Of course, there's a chance this might not work. But it seems more productive than a stakeout. And if it doesn't do the trick, we can always go to Plan B."

"What's Plan B?" asked Ray.

Rachel smiled. "A stakeout."

"Sounds fine to me," said Trip. The others quickly agreed.

"Great," said Rachel. "Wendy and I will go get the dune buggies. You guys can set up something to monitor the screen, then get back to work on Sherlock."

"SETBACK!"

The word was written in large, shaky letters that covered an entire page of the fanatic's journal.

Jaws clenched, eyes steely, she stared at the page for a while. Then she turned it over and began to write in smaller letters at the top of the next page:

"My plans have been delayed. This is upsetting, but not entirely bad. After all, the reason for the delay is of my own doing. I have broadened my goals, and as a result, it will take me longer than I had expected to complete my preparations.

"The delay will be worth it, for the end result will be far greater than I had initially dared to dream."

She paused and stared straight ahead. The room was dark, the wall bare. But to her fevered eyes it was like a movie screen, where the action she was considering could be played over and over again, savored in all its fearful glory.

It started with a package—a simple package no bigger than a man's head.

A package placed in just the right location.

And then there was the timer. It would tell the package *when* to do its job.

And then there would be the explosion, a slow blossoming of fire and terror that would rip through the island, breaking it into a billion tiny pieces. So many pieces they could never be put back together again.

The fanatic could picture it down to the last detail.

"It's a good feeling, this knowing what one has to do. I am at peace with the world now. I actually feel happy, knowing I will do something important before I die.

"And I *will* have to die to accomplish this. Everyone on the island has to die. It took me a while to realize that. But the truth is that simply destroying the computer is not enough. It could be built again. Instead I must destroy the fools who would create such a monstrosity to begin with.

"So my bomb must be far more powerful than I first realized, lest this devil machine have a chance to be born again.

"For that reason, I see now that this delay is not really a setback at all, but a step forward. It is upsetting only because I am so eager to carry out my holy task. But I can wait, I must wait, until I can make sure that the bomb is great enough, powerful enough, to do what must be done. . . ."

"Hi, guys!" yelled Paracelsus, when Wendy and Rachel came through the door. "I'm watching the screen for you."

131

Rachel gave her brother a questioning look.

"I put him in front of the monitor," said Roger. "Then I got him to focus on the red circle that represents our friend's computer. Then I programmed him to yell bloody murder if it began to blink."

"Bloody murder!" yelled Paracelsus. *"Bloody murder!"*

The group ran into the room where Paracelsus was keeping watch.

"Heh-heh-heh," chuckled the bronze head. "I just wanted to see if you were paying attention."

"Roger!" cried Rachel and Wendy together.

"What are you looking at me for?" asked Roger, his face the picture of wounded innocence. "It was Paracelsus who called you in here."

"Yeah," said Wendy, "but unless there's been some great breakthrough in programming that will let him think for himself, it was you who put the words in his mouth."

Roger smiled. "Guilty as charged. But I'd like to point out something: You all reacted just as I expected you would."

"What do you mean?" asked Trip.

"You ran in here."

"So?"

"So what good does it do us to run in here? What we should do when Paracelsus sounds the alarm is head straight for the dune buggies so we can catch the mad messenger before he or she has a chance

to get out of that house again. If that had been a real alarm, the time we wasted running in to check the screen might have meant the difference between catching this guy and losing him."

"You've got a point," said Wendy reluctantly.

"Yes," said Paracelsus. "But the way he combs his hair covers it up."

"What did you use to program him?" asked Ray. "Old joke books?"

"As a matter of fact, we did," said Rachel. "At least, one of us did." She looked at Roger meaningfully.

"It's part of the chatter factor I mentioned," said Roger.

"That brings up an idea I had for Sherlock," said Trip. "I call it the random factor."

"Sounds interesting," said Wendy. "What do you have in mind?"

"Well, we're going to make this a highly logical program, right?"

Everyone nodded their agreement.

"Okay, that's fine as far as it goes. But it seems to me that that very logicalness might be one of the limitations of a thinking machine. One of the things that makes humans different from computers is the way our brains are built. A computer has a massive memory, and it can get at anything in there—but usually only in a very structured, very formal way.

"Now think about the human brain. We have a

massive memory, too, only we don't always realize it because we can't always get stuff back out when we want it. According to my father, everything we ever experience is stored away in part of the brain called the subconscious."

"I thought your mother was the scientist," said Roger.

"She is. My father is an artist. But if you don't think artists are interested in the way the brain works, you've got another think coming. Dad has spent a lot of time studying creativity—which is what I was coming around to.

"The problem with human memory is we can't always get at stuff when we want it. It's like having files in your computer that you can't access. But what does happen down there is that things scramble around, kind of bumping into each other. That's why your dreams are so weird, such a jumble of images. It's also one of the ways fresh ideas are born: the under-brain putting old things together in new ways.

"That's why some of the most brilliant thinkers get their best ideas in dreams. The things running around down in the bottom of their brains have connected in some new and exciting way."

"What does this have to do with the computer?" asked Wendy.

"Well, why can't we program Sherlock that way? Should we have him use logic? Of course. But how about programming him to try illogical solutions to problems, too? He might just end up being brilliant!"

No one said anything for a moment as they tried to digest what Trip had been telling them.

It was Paracelsus who broke the silence.

"Bloody murder!" he screamed. "Bloody murder."

The kids pulled their dune buggies to a stop about a hundred yards from the house. Even though the engines were almost completely silent, they didn't want to chance the sound of a wheel on gravel alerting their quarry.

"Trip, you and Wendy circle around to the far side of the house," said Roger. "Let's not lose this dude through the back door."

The two blonds, one towering over the other, moved quietly but rapidly through the long row of bushes that bordered the back lawns of the abandoned houses.

Roger glanced at Ray and Rachel.

They nodded their readiness.

As he began to lead them forward, Roger found himself wishing the group had thought this through a little further. What were they going to do with this character if they caught him? Should they actually go into the house and try to detain him? Or would it be enough just to try to get a look at whoever it was and then go to Dr. Hwa?

Roger supposed if someone was fooling around

with the computer, Dr. Hwa should know about it. On the other hand, he didn't like the idea of asking anyone else to handle their problems.

Yet they had no idea whether this person was actually dangerous or not. Were the threatening messages just a prank—or the work of some dangerous lunatic?

The muscles in Roger's shoulders were so tight he was afraid he would get a cramp. His palms were soaked with sweat. Flanked by Rachel and Ray, he stood looking at the house for what seemed an eternity. What if the message sender had already left?

Before Roger could decide whether they should go into the house, the matter was taken out of his hands.

The front door swung open and the boy named Hap, the dune buggy driver Trip had nearly collided with the day before, stepped out. "Well," he said with a smile. "It's about time. I wondered when you were going to catch me!"

14

Explanations =
More Mysteries!

THE BABBLE OF VOICES THAT GREETED HAP'S CA-
sual reaction to being discovered made it impossible to think. Trip and Wendy arriving from the
other side of the house only added to the confusion.

"All right, all right, everybody shut up!" bellowed Roger at last.

In the silence that followed he took a step toward
the other boy, eyeing him warily, as if he still expected him to run—or even attack.

"Hey, I'm not going anywhere," said Hap. "You
caught me, fair and square." He spread his hands
and laughed. "Now the question is—what are you
going to do with me?"

Roger scowled. What *could* they do with him?

Tell his parents? They didn't even know who his parents were. Of course, they could turn him in to Dr. Hwa. But it would be better if they could handle the situation on their own. "We're not going to do anything with you," he said at last. "We just want some answers."

"Fair enough. I'll trade you answer for answer."

"No," said Roger. "Right now you owe us a few."

Hap shrugged. "We'll see. Why don't we go inside where we can all sit down?"

Roger glanced at the other members of the gang and realized they were waiting for him to make the decision. He looked back at Hap and wondered if this was a trap of some kind.

"Coming?"

Roger decided to take the chance. "All right. Lead the way."

The inside of the house had been stripped when the officer who last lived there had left the island. With no furniture the empty rooms seemed unusually large—and slightly eerie.

"Too neat," said Wendy, looking around. "I prefer a healthy dose of clutter."

A flicker of annoyance passed over their host's face. "Have a seat," he said, gesturing to the floor.

Nobody moved.

The boy shrugged, then lowered himself so that he was sitting cross-legged on the floor.

"What's your name?" asked Roger.

"Hap."

"We know that," snapped Trip. "Hap who?"

"Swenson."

A look passed between the other kids.

Ray pushed his glasses up onto his nose with the tip of his forefinger. "You're not Mr. Swenson's son, are you?"

"Someone's in for a rude surprise if I'm not."

Trip groaned.

"Why did you send us those messages?" asked Rachel, sliding down the wall into a squatting position.

Hap shrugged. "I was bored. And you people were so wrapped up in yourselves you barely noticed I existed, except to stare at me once in a while as if I was a spy or something. I never saw such a stuck-up group."

Rachel blushed. Their less-than-generous treatment of this boy when he served them in the canteen had been pricking her conscience as it was. His words confirmed what she had suspected, and brought her feelings of guilt to full flower.

Those words obviously weren't having the same effect on Wendy. "Oh, bullfeathers!" she exclaimed. "We had things to talk about. You were the waiter. I don't believe in abusing the help, but I'm not going to feel guilty because we didn't decide we couldn't live without you!"

Hap turned away, his face sullen. An awkward silence fell over the room. It was finally broken when Trip folded his long legs, sank to the floor with Rachel and Hap, and asked, "So how did you do it?"

"Send the messages?"

Trip nodded.

Hap looked a little nervous. "When the Air Force pulled out, they left terminals in a lot of the houses. It wasn't too much work to reconnect the thing."

"That's not the issue," said Roger, rubbing his thumb and forefinger together furiously. "And you know it." He looked Hap straight in the eye. "Each of our terminals has an access code that should be virtually impossible to break. But you did it. How?"

"I don't know."

The others stared at him. "I beg your pardon?" said Roger.

"I don't know," repeated Hap, looking even more nervous. "I was just hacking around, not really expecting anything to happen, when I made contact with your terminals." He took a deep breath. "I hadn't really been planning to send a message, but I was still mad, and when the chance came up . . ." He shrugged, leaving the sentence unfinished. "The thing is, I shouldn't have been able to do that. It scared me a little."

Hap looked at the circle of faces surrounding him. He seemed to be trying to decide whether he should say the next thing on his mind. "If you want to know the truth," he said at last, "I think someone has been tampering with the system."

"Yeah," said Ray. "You."

"Don't be stupid! I was just playing with a terminal. I think someone else has fiddled with the mainframe's security program."

"I want to go home," said Wendy. "This place is
Weirdsville."

Roger began pacing back and forth, rubbing his
thumb and forefinger together faster than before.
"Weirdsville is right. But you can bet that we're
not going anywhere, so we'd better start putting
things together to see if we can make sense out of
them. I wish Sherlock was up and running."

"Sherlock?" asked Hap.

Roger paused. Should they trust this newcomer?

He looked at the others. Again they were leaving
the decision up to him. Again he decided to take
the chance.

"Sherlock is a program we're trying to create,"
he said, settling to the floor. "What we're shooting
for is an A.I. crimesolver."

Though he had decided to trust Hap, he deliber-
ately held back on telling him how big their plans
really were. The idea that they were trying to create
a self-aware computer was not something he was
ready to share with a newcomer to the group. It
was only then that he realized that despite the fact
that they had been enemies, he was indeed considering Hap as a possible member of the gang.

"The original idea was to get something that
would help us figure out some of the weird things
that have been happening here," explained Rachel.

"You sound like there were more weird things than my messages," said Hap.

"Well, there was that explosion at the guard shack," said Ray.

Hap shrugged. "My father says that was just an accident."

"Could be," said Trip. "Personally, I'm not ready to toss it off that easily."

"And then there was the bug," said Rachel.

"Bug?"

Quickly Rachel filled him in on the details of the microphone that had been planted on her collar. When she was done, he let out a low whistle. "That *is* weird."

"Especially when you consider that it was almost certainly planted by one of the adults at that meeting," said Rachel.

"But why?"

"That's what we want to know!" exclaimed Wendy. "Actually, it was what first got us started on Operation Sherlock. But things just keep getting weirder. For example last night Dr. Remov was telling us that he was worried about some spy group called G.H.O.S.T."

"And there's the fact that we never got in trouble for denting the dune buggy," put in Trip. "Don't forget about that."

Hap began to laugh. "Well, that's one mystery I can solve for you. I took care of it. I got one of the mechanics to help me, and we had the whole thing looking good as new before my father had a clue that anything had happened. Those new snap-in panels are great. We could never have done it fast enough without them."

"But *why* did you do it?" asked Trip, looking astonished.

Hap smiled. "A couple of reasons. For one thing, I figured if I ever did get to know you guys, I would just as soon you still have the use of the duners. I didn't want to be stuck bombing around all alone out there! And to tell you the truth, I felt a little guilty. Despite what I said, the accident was at least half my fault."

"No," said Trip. "It was mostly my fault. I should have been more careful."

"Let's not get too mushy," said Wendy. "I have a delicate stomach. Besides, that only clears up one mystery, and one of the smaller ones at that. We've still got some real weirdness left to deal with."

"Let's run through it again," said Roger. "We've cleared up the mysterious messages and the self-regenerating dune buggy. But there's still"—(he began ticking things off on his fingers as he spoke)—"one, the explosion. Two, the bug on Rachel's collar. Three, the fact that Hap was doing things on the computer that he simply shouldn't have been *able* to do." He paused, then said, "Three strikes and you're out. I think it's time we went to see Dr. Hwa."

15

A Visit to Dr. Hwa

HAP STOOD WITH THE GANG OUTSIDE THE HUGE marble building that held the main offices for Project Alpha. His mother had excused him from working in the canteen for the afternoon so that he could come along with the group. She had no idea what they were up to—she was just so relieved he had made some friends that she was more than happy to give him the time off.

He felt funny being with the others after the tension that had existed between them. They were certainly trying to be polite to him now, Rachel especially. But it was clear that they were not entirely comfortable with him; particularly the one they called the Wonderchild.

I wonder if I would have been invited along if I didn't have important evidence to add? he thought—and then immediately began to worry about having to tell Dr. Hwa about what he had been up to.

His fussing was interrupted by Roger. "All right, are we clear on our strategy?" he asked, speaking to the group as a whole. "We don't want to look like a bunch of idiots, so unless Dr. Hwa specifically asks one of us something, we'll stick with the things we decided. I'll start by explaining why we're here. Rachel will talk about the transmitter on her collar. Then Hap will tell why he thinks the computer has been tampered with. If it comes up, Ray can mention that we're still not convinced that the explosion at the guard shack was an accident. Trip and Wendy, you can verify things for us, but for the time being you don't have any major data to present. Got it?"

They all nodded.

"Then let's go."

Funny, thought Trip. *I'd be nervous as a cat in a dog pound if I were doing this on my own. But with all of us together, it doesn't bother me at all.*

They had to sign in at the front desk, where they were given little plastic badges embedded with a microchip that would set off an alarm if they ventured into any restricted areas. The receptionist pointed the way to Dr. Hwa's office.

It didn't take long before they met their first real obstacle: Bridget McGrory.

"Saints preserve us!" cried the fiery Irishwoman

when the kids presented themselves at her desk. "What is this? A research project or a day-care center? No, you can't see Dr. Hwa. He's busy! Now, get on with you!"

"But it's urgent," said Roger.

"It's urgent that you rascals get yourselves out of here," snapped the formidable Ms. McGrory. "I've got work to do."

"Now, look, Toots," said Wendy. "I don't—"

She was interrupted by the door to the inner office swinging open. "What's the commotion, Bridget?" asked a quiet voice.

"There, now." The secretary sighed, exasperation heavy in her voice. "You've gone and disturbed Himself. I'm sorry, Dr. Hwa. These scamps were trying to get in to see you."

"These 'scamps' are welcome here anytime," said Dr. Hwa softly. He gave his secretary a wink. "Let's not take ourselves so seriously, Bridget."

Ignoring her scowl, he turned to the gang and said, "Come right in. I'm eager to talk to you."

Feeling smug, the kids filed into Hwa's office.

Ray, who was last in line, tripped over his shoelace on the way. As he was picking himself up, he noticed Bridget McGrory reaching under her desk. When the secretary saw him watching her, she jerked her hand back as if she had been burned.

"Get on with you!" she snapped. "Now that

you've interrupted him, don't keep the doctor waiting!"

Ray scurried into the office. *What was that all about?* he wondered as he closed the door behind him.

Dr. Hwa's office—his *sanctum sanctorum,* as he referred to it—was an elegant combination of beautifully patterned oriental carpets, real walnut paneling, and highly polished desks and conference tables. Several Chinese-style landscapes hung on the wall behind his desk.

Dr. Hwa himself was dressed in a white lab coat. Taking a seat on the corner of the desk, he listened intently to what the gang had come to tell him. His brow was creased, and he looked worried.

"You say this microphone, this 'bug,' disintegrated after you took it off Rachel's collar?"

Rachel nodded.

"Then how do you know it was a microphone? I'm not saying it wasn't, mind you. But I need to know."

"What else could it have been?" asked Ray indignantly.

Dr. Hwa shrugged. "I don't know. I didn't see it. I'm just asking."

Roger began to fidget uneasily. This wasn't going the way he had planned. "But Hap's messages . . ." he began.

"Ah, yes." Dr. Hwa looked severe. "The messages. I must say, I am a little disappointed. I gave you youngsters access to a magnificent computer in hopes that you would use it constructively. These silly games of annoying one another . . ." He shook his head sadly. "Well, youth will be youth, I suppose. But let's have no more of this, shall we?"

"But the messages," repeated Roger. "Hap should never have been able to get them through to our terminals."

"A simple glitch," said Dr. Hwa. "And one we were already aware of. In fact, I wager if you had tried one of your pranks this afternoon, Mr. Swenson, you would have found yourself blocked." Dr. Hwa gave Hap a wink. "I would suggest that we keep this all to ourselves," he said. "No sense in alarming the others."

By which it was clear that he meant he would not tell Hap's father what Hap had been up to.

"Yes," said Hap gratefully. "I think that's a good idea, Dr. Hwa."

"I thought you would. Now, if you will excuse me . . ."

"But Dr. Hwa!" cried Roger.

"Yes?"

The redhead paused. The doctor had effectively dismantled all their arguments. "Nothing," he said glumly. "Thanks for taking the time to talk to us."

"Think nothing of it. Come and see me anytime you like. I'll tell our Ms. McGrory not to protect me from you quite so zealously in the future." He flashed them a conspiratorial smile, then sobered a bit. "I will warn you, though: I am often in the lab. If that is the case, you will not be able to get to me. I allow *nothing* to disturb me while I am working."

The ferocity with which he said this made it clear that when it came to his work, the little scientist was dead serious.

After the failure of their meeting with Dr. Hwa, the gang decided there was only one thing to do: proceed full speed ahead with Operation Sherlock.

Which was just what they did. When they decided they needed even more privacy than the Phillips house could provide, Hap suggested that they move their base of operations to the abandoned house from which he had been sending them messages.

Soon they were gathering there every morning, when they would meet to discuss their strategy for the day.

Hap himself turned out to be an unexpectedly strong addition to the group. While he lacked the programming skills the others had picked up from their parents, he was a superb "nuts and bolts" person. When Rachel suggested they add a voice synthesizer to the terminal, it was Hap who cobbled together the parts to make it. When they wanted to add extra keyboards to the workstation so that more than one of them could input things at the same time, it was Hap who figured out the most efficient way to do the wiring.

Operation Sherlock began to progress rapidly as each of them added to it from their own strengths. Before long they had the computer conversing with them in a limited fashion—in much the same manner as Paracelsus, though with more serious intent. (It was Roger's idea to give the computer's voice a British accent in order to make its speech patterns reflect the way the original Sherlock Holmes would have sounded. It was Ray who got his movie-buff father to loan them a voice pattern for Basil Rathbone, the actor who had played Holmes in so many old films.)

Each of them contributed to the project in his or her own fashion. The Gamma Ray, for example, turned out to be a superb "glitch spotter." When an addition to the program seemed perfect but just wouldn't run, more often than not it was Ray who could find the tiny mistake that was causing the major problem. Before long he had pinned a score sheet on the wall next to his workstation where he kept a tally of the glitches he had successfully zapped.

Roger and Rachel were the primary information programmers. Drawing on their own vast pool of knowledge, they spent much of their time simply adding to Sherlock's store of general information. When the others found out how many hard facts the twins carried in their heads, they came to be considered the gang's walking data base. It was a rare occasion when someone asked a factual question that one or the other of them couldn't answer.

Trip tended to work with spurts of inspiration, leaping past logic to unconventional solutions that were often highly effective. The thrill of those moments made up for the long, frustrating hours that he spent staring at the keyboard or some manual without making any progress at all.

Sometimes he alleviated the frustration of those dry spells by going out on a "scrounge" to turn up materials the gang needed for various aspects of their project. Ray usually accompanied him, and the two of them were remarkably adept at turning up all kinds of useful junk.

As for Wendy and Hap, to everyone's surprise they quickly formed a good working team. By pooling the Wonderchild's ability to miniaturize with Hap's skills at putting things together, they were able to make highly effective additions to the abandoned terminal. In a short time it was a far more sophisticated piece of hardware than any of the ones that had been installed in their own homes.

They found themselves falling into a pleasant schedule. They would work like crazy all morning, then around noon each day jump into their dune buggies and head for the beach, where they would have a picnic and take a leisurely swim before returning to the project. They gained a new pleasure when Hap found a security guard named Max who was willing to give them scuba lessons. Soon they were meeting Max every other day—usually late in the afternoon—for instruction.

They even discovered a cavern one day when they were hiking in the steep hills at the north end of the island. It was at the base of one of the hills, about a quarter of a mile in from the coast. "This is so cool!" said Trip enthusiastically as they began to clear brush from the entrance. "I bet no one else even knows this is here."

"You're probably right," agreed Hap as they stepped inside. "I'm pretty sure I would have heard about this if anyone did know it was here." He looked around admiringly. "This would be a great place to hide out!"

Evenings they gathered at the canteen to plan their next day's work and play a few rounds of Gamma Ball. Once they even organized a tournament with some of the island staffers.

All in all it was a happy time for the gang—save for one thing: Even though nothing unusual had happened for some time, none of them could escape the nagging feeling that they were working against a deadline.

That feeling was made all the more frustrating because they didn't know when the deadline was.

They found out the night Hap, Trip, and Ray crossed paths with the fanatic.

16

The Bomb

It had started out to be a good day. Wendy and Hap, wanting a break from their work on Sherlock, had combined their skills to put together something else they felt the gang needed: a personal communication system.

"Hey, you guys, come get a load of this!" yelled Wendy, late in the morning.

"It's only a prototype," said Hap modestly when the others had gathered around them. "But if it works we'll clean up the design a bit and make one for each of us."

"Make one what?" asked Trip. "I still don't know what it is."

"A miniaturized walkie-talkie, you towering turkey," said Wendy. "You wear it on your wrist."

"Shades of Dick Tracy!" cried Roger.

"If you're going to make fun of them, you don't

have to wear one," snapped Wendy. She looked hurt.

"Who's making fun?" asked Roger. "I love that comic strip. But you have to admit they had the idea first. Which is no reason for *us* not to have them. I think it's a great idea."

Wendy searched Roger's face for any sign of sarcasm. "Okay," she said finally. A little suspicion still clung to her voice. She had already had enough teasing in her life from people who didn't matter. She really didn't want it from these kids whom she had come to feel so close to.

"So how does it work?" asked Trip, deciding it was time to change the subject.

"To begin with, it operates underneath the island's electronic shield," said Wendy.

"We built in a pretty wide range of options," continued Hap. "For example, you can ring up someone else if you have their code number. Actually, in some ways its more like a wristwatch-sized telephone than the old Dick Tracy wrist radios. The biggest problem right now is that their range is only about a mile and a half. But we figured they might come in handy anyway."

"Miniaturizing them has been brutal," said Wendy. "We've only got two finished so far. But that's enough for a trial run. Want to go see if they work?"

The suggestion met with instant approval, and within five minutes the gang had divided into two groups. Leaving their headquarters, they started in opposite directions to test the clarity and range of the new devices.

Trip and the twins headed north. The trio's heads made an oddly colorful triangle, with Trip's buttery blond hair centered between about a foot above Roger and Rachel's fiery crowns.

Wendy, Hap, and Ray headed south, Wendy and Ray as short compared to Hap as the twins were to their companion. Since they would be passing the recreation area, Ray was clutching his basketball, which he brought to headquarters each morning, even though he couldn't get anyone to play with him. He was trying to dribble the ball as they walked, without notable success.

"Why don't you take up a new game?" asked Wendy. "One where you don't have anything you can drop so often. Checkers, for example."

"Laugh," said Ray. "Make fun. But when I get the hang of this, I'll be terribly short but great on the court. You'll just be short."

"Whoa!" cried Hap, grabbing Wendy as she launched herself at the Gamma Ray. "Let's keep it cerebral."

"Okay, okay," said Wendy, squirming her way out of Hap's grasp. "But I'm not in a very good mood today. Another short joke and the Gamma Ray is gonna hit a lead wall."

"Who's making short jokes?" asked a voice behind them. It didn't stay behind them long, because its owner was jogging, and in another second had run past them. It was Dr. Fontana. Jogging along next to her, ebony pigtails flouncing back and forth, was the beautiful Dr. Ling.

Ray dropped his basketball.

"Watch the short jokes!" cried Dr. Fontana over her shoulder. "We little people have to stick together!"

"Yeah," said Ray bitterly, picking up his basketball. "Stick enough of us together and you can make a regular-size person."

"I feel like I've been stranded in a world of pygmies," said Hap, once the women were out of hearing range.

"Watch the short jokes!" cried Wendy and Ray together.

Before Hap could respond, the device strapped to his wrist began to crackle. "All in!" said a voice that sounded vaguely like Roger's. "All in!"

"All in?" asked Wendy. "What the heck is he talking about?"

Hap pressed a couple of buttons on the side of the device. "Hap to Roger. Hap to Roger. What are you saying?"

"Aunt Eeroo," replied Roger.

"Now he's talking about his relatives," said Wendy. "Here, give me that."

"All right, all right!" said Hap, peeling Wendy's hand off his wrist. "Let me keep some skin, will you?"

"Aunt Eeroo," said Roger again.

Hap passed the wrist radio to Wendy, who fiddled with some of the buttons.

"Roger, this is Wendy. Come in, Roger."

"Ill Aunt Eeroo," crackled back Roger's voice.

"Now his aunt's sick," said Wendy, her voice thick with disgust. "These things are worthless. Come on, let's head back to the house."

"Maybe that's what he meant by 'All in!' " suggested Ray.

Hap shrugged. Wendy said nothing. She had worked hard on the communicators, and though she didn't want to show it, she was bitterly disappointed that they functioned so poorly.

"What in heaven's name were you trying to say to us?" asked Hap when they rejoined the others at the house.

"Well, I started with 'Calling in,' " said Roger. "But all I got back was a bunch of static from your device."

"We kept hearing 'All in!' " said Ray. "I thought you were trying to get us to come back to headquarters. And who's your Aunt Eeroo?"

Roger began to laugh. "Probably that's what you got when I kept shouting, 'Can't hear you!' "

"Give me those things," snapped Wendy. "I've got work to do."

Snatching the wrist radios from Roger and Hap, she stationed herself at her corner work desk, where she began working on the devices with the help of a screwdriver no bigger than a sewing needle. She punctuated her efforts with several words that probably didn't have any effect at all, but seemed to make her feel better.

Instead of gathering at the canteen that night, or watching a film at Ray's house, as they often did (Ray's father being a notorious fan of monster movies), the gang met again at their hideout.

After a few more hours of fiddling with the communicators, Wendy came over to where the others were working on Sherlock.

"Ask it a question," said Roger proudly.

Wendy shrugged. "How many square miles on Anza-bora Island?"

The computer made no response.

"Oops," said Roger. "I forgot to tell you, you have to start a question with 'Sherlock.' That's the access code—it let's the computer know you're talking to it."

"Okay," said Wendy. "Sherlock, how many square miles in Anza-bora Island?"

"The answer is elementary," said the computer in a crisp British accent.

"Listen to that voice!" cried Roger. "Those tones, that accent! Isn't it great? He sounds just like Sherlock Holmes would have."

"Impressive," said Wendy. "But I notice I still didn't get an answer to my question."

Roger shrugged. "You can't have everything."

"Well, given my choice, I'd go for silent but useful," snapped Wendy.

"It's been a long day," said Rachel, sensing trouble. "Maybe we'd better call it quits for now."

Wendy flopped into a beanbag chair one of them had brought from their home. "You're right, Rach. I couldn't get those wrist things to work the way I want and it's made me nasty. I apologize to all of you. Even you, Sherlock."

"Thank you," said the computer. "It was elementary."

Hap and Trip moved fast enough to grab Wendy before she could throw the beanbag chair at the terminal.

Operation Sherlock was being created at a terminal tied to the island's main computer.

Even as the gang worked at that terminal, tapping into the computer's power and abilities, a woman with glittering eyes crouched at the frozen heart of the computer itself. Holding her breath, she made one final adjustment to a small timer, and then began to grin.

With the bomb finally in place, the fanatic felt as if a huge burden had been lifted from the weary shoulders that had carried it for so long. She let out a sigh that bloomed into a small cloud of steam.

It was hard to understand how everyone else could be so blind. Why didn't they see what a menace this computer was? Why didn't they see that someone had to take action?

That knowledge was a terrible weight to carry alone. It was so hard being the only one who could see clearly, the only one who could sense the danger. That understanding had preyed heavily on the fanatic's sense of responsibility.

Now those worries were gone.

"I have to save the world from the computer," was the phrase most often repeated in her journal. "I have to save the world."

Now, at last, the world *was* saved. Or at least, soon would be.

The fanatic patted the bulky package that would do the job. It hadn't really been necessary to plant the bomb right here at the heart of the computer. It was such an improvement over her first feeble attempts that if it went off anywhere on the island, it would destroy the evil mechanical brain. Yet somehow it seemed appropriate—poetic, almost— to position the bomb right inside the vile machine.

Trying to move the deadly package more securely into place, she pushed aside a handful of cables and wires. Four of them were connected to the secret transmitter Black Glove had previously attached to the other side of the support post where the bomb was now being installed.

The fanatic frowned. The bomb still wasn't sitting properly. Shivering now, impatient, she moved the wires again. In the process, she completely disconnected Black Glove's secret device.

A few minutes more and the job was done. The fanatic lingered briefly, then sighed and moved away. It was hard to leave this scene of triumph, but it was too cold to stay. Besides, even though the timer had been set for well past midnight and there were several hours left before the blast would tear the island to pieces, she still had much to do to get ready for the end.

Ducking under a crossbar, the fanatic left the heart of the computer.

Left alone, the bomb continued marking off the seconds until it would destroy Anza-bora Island and everyone on it.

Wrapping up their work for the day, the gang headed in different directions. Wendy, pleading exhaustion, planned to go straight home. The twins, who had not yet started a job they had promised their father they would finish before morning, decided that home was the safest bet for them, too.

Hap, Trip, and Ray opted to head for the canteen, with the idea of getting in a few rounds of Gamma Ball before they went to bed. As it turned out, they got carried away with their game and didn't notice the time until it was almost midnight.

"Holy Moses!" cried Ray when he glanced at his watch. "My parents are going to kill me!"

"Mine, too!" cried Trip in dismay. "I should have been home an hour ago."

Mrs. Swenson, who had been working silently behind the counter, said, "Hap, why not ask your friends to spend the night at our place? The three of you can start for home now. I'll meet you there when I'm done closing up here."

Hap looked at the others questioningly.

"That sounds great, Mrs. Swenson," said Ray. "But my parents . . ."

"I'll call your folks and take care of everything," said Mrs. Swenson with a wink. "Yours, too, Trip."

"It's a deal," said Trip.

Hap smiled. "Thanks, Mom."

Silently he made a vow to give his mother some extra help the next day. He had already been feeling pangs of guilt because she had been stuck with almost all the canteen work since he had made friends with the gang. Though she claimed she was glad to have him spend the time with kids his own age, Hap decided he had better start making some of that up to her.

"You can stay out on the beach for a while if you want," called Mrs. Swenson as the boys headed for the door. "Just don't be too late."

"You bet," said Hap.

Giving Mrs. Swenson a wave, the three boys left the canteen.

They were passing the computer center a few

minutes later when they saw a tall figure in a lab coat slip through the side door.

"That's funny," said Hap. "They should have been done working hours ago."

"Are you kidding?" asked Trip. "These scientists work whenever the mood hits them. My mother usually stays up all night when a project is really cooking." He squinted at the figure. "I can't tell who that is. It's too dark out."

"Maybe it's the spy!" said Ray.

"Could be," said Hap quietly. "Look at the way he—no, I think it's a she—is walking." Taking the others by the arms, he drew them behind a bush. "That is not the walk of an innocent person. See how she keeps checking back and forth? She doesn't want to be seen."

Indeed, the woman was constantly looking around as if to spot any possible enemies.

"Maybe she's just nervous," said Ray softly.

"Could be," said Hap. "But I think we're on to something. I vote we do a little tailing."

Ray and Trip glanced at each other, than back at the skulking figure. "All right," said Trip. "I'm game."

"Me, too," whispered Ray, pushing his glasses back up onto the bridge of his nose.

Hap put his hand on the others' shoulders and drew them back as the woman headed in their direction. A slight sea breeze rustled the leaves on the bush behind which they were hiding. In the distance they could hear the ocean.

"Now," whispered Hap when their quarry was far enough ahead of them.

Without making a sound, the three boys slipped from behind the bush. Clinging to the shadows themselves, they followed the mysterious figure down the road.

17

Death Trap

THE NIGHT WAS CLOUDY, THE MOON HANGING OVER Anza-bora Island a mere sliver. The Gamma Ray stifled a groan as he stumbled over a rock and fell to his knees. It was the third fall he had taken since they began trailing the mystery woman. He needed more light!

While Hap scooted ahead so as not to lose sight of their quarry, Trip bent to help Ray up. He shivered as he did so. The salty wind blowing in from the ocean was cold.

"I think she's on to us," whispered Ray, once he was back on his feet.

"Why?"

"She's trying to shake us. We haven't gone in a circle yet, but we've been making some awfully big loops. I can't think of a reason for anyone to take this route, except to try to dump us."

* * *

Ahead of them, the woman glanced over her shoulder and cursed. Whoever was back there was hanging on.

Why don't they leave me alone? she thought anxiously. *I don't want to hurt anyone.*

To her troubled mind, blowing up an entire island and all the people on it was utterly different from taking steps to prevent two or three individuals from sounding the alarm. That could involve harming someone personally!

Still, they could not be allowed to jeopardize the mission. . . .

About a hundred yards behind the fanatic, Trip and Ray pulled Hap to a stop.

"She's figured out someone is following her," whispered Ray, when Hap protested and tried to break free of them. "Let's hold back a bit and see if we can convince her she's lost us."

"If we hold back we *will* lose her!" hissed Hap, shrugging himself out of their grip.

"Hap's right," said Trip to Ray. "You're both right. I don't know what to do."

"You two hang back," suggested Hap. "I know the terrain better, so I can do the trailing less conspicuously. I'll keep track of the suspect—you keep track of me."

"Good enough," whispered Ray. "Go for it!"

Hap sprinted ahead of them. In seconds he had blended into the night landscape.

"He's good," whispered Trip. "She'll never spot him. The problem is, I can't, either! I don't have the slightest idea where he went!"

Just then a stone landed at Trip's feet.

"It came from that way!" hissed Ray.

Following Hap's lead, they scurried into the darkness.

Are they gone?

The fanatic stopped to listen. Not a sound came through the darkness.

She frowned. Whoever was following her had been clinging to the trail so tenaciously it hardly seemed possible she had lost them. Yet there didn't seem to be anyone back there.

Wait!

A footstep on gravel. Soft, slow, infinitely patient. But definitely there.

The fanatic's frown grew harsher, deeper. *All right, you asked for it. Now we play for keeps.*

It worked! thought Hap. *Look how careless she's getting.*

Indeed, the figure that had flitted so elusively through the night now seemed calm and confident, as if thoroughly convinced no one was following it.

Still moving cautiously, Hap kept his quarry in sight while trying to get a chance to motion Trip and Ray to join him. The moment came, and before long the other two were at his side.

"I think we're home free," whispered Hap. "She seems to have relaxed. If we can stay quiet, I think she'll lead us right to her den."

It wasn't long before their destination became clear.

"The power plant!" whispered Ray.

"Do you suppose she's the one who blew up the guard shack?" asked Trip nervously.

"Maybe she's planning to blow up the whole power plant," said Hap.

"I think we ought to get help," said Ray.

"I'd agree, if I thought anyone would believe us," replied Trip. "But remember what happened when we tried to tell Dr. Hwa about our suspicions? We need more proof before we can do anything about this. Besides, just because she's acting suspicious, doesn't mean she's actually doing anything wrong. Heck, anyone following us would think that *we* were acting suspicious!"

"But I don't think we should just drop this," said Hap.

"I agree," said Trip. "Let's follow her for a while longer."

Though the crater left by the guard shack explosion had been repaired some time earlier, the fence was still in place. However, it had not been locked for several days. The boys waited until their quarry was a fair distance down the road, then slipped through the gate.

*   *   *

The door to the power plant was open when they got there. They realized later that that should have clued them in that all was not right. But they were too close to the prey now; the hunting instinct overcame all common sense.

They entered the office.

The second door, leading into the plant itself, was open, too. They headed straight for it.

As they passed through that door, the first door—the door to the outside—swung silently shut.

A shadowy hand twisted a key in the lock.

The trap was sealed; the hunted had become the hunter.

The three boys passed into the power plant. The slender crescent moon was directly overhead. Its dim light filtered through the glass ceiling, making weird shadows of the tall arms that ranged the length of the great enclosed space.

"I wish we had more light," whispered Ray. "I can't see a thing."

As if to prove it, he stumbled over something on the floor and fell to his hands and knees.

While Trip helped Ray to his feet, Hap looked up and down the power plant. "That woman could be anywhere in here," he whispered, awed by the plant's size and complexity.

The hint of fear in his voice made Ray and Trip more nervous than they already were.

The tide was out. The top edges of the great

boxes used to harness the ocean's power rested at floor level, their recently cleaned lids still wide open.

"Should we split up to search?" asked Hap.

"No!" hissed Ray. "Let's stick together."

They did just that, looking almost like a three-headed being as they moved forward into the plant.

Without a sound the woman they had been trailing slid to the control panel that had been demonstrated to Trip and Ray several days before.

All it took was a tap on one of the buttons. . . .

"What was that?" whispered Trip.

The sound had come from one of the great tide boxes. The fanatic had made the lid jump a bit—just enough to attract the boys' attention.

"It came from over there," said Ray.

Still clustered together the boys moved forward to investigate. The sound of the ocean, its waves lapping under the back wall of the building, masked their footsteps—but also made it difficult for them to hear what anyone else might be doing.

The fanatic stood trembling at the control panel. *Just a bit farther. Just a bit farther . . .*

"Are these the boxes you told me about?" asked Hap, peering over the edge into a great Plexiglass cubicle. It was hard to see in the dim light.

Just a bit farther . . .

Trip and Ray joined Hap at the edge of the box. "That's one of them," confirmed Trip.

Close enough!

The fanatic punched a pair of buttons. The ten-foot-square grilles that covered the boxes to the left and right of the boys slammed shut with thunderous force. The speed was incredible, the noise deafening. At the same time the fanatic let out a bloodcurdling scream and brought a row of lights flaring into life.

Aside from the whisper of the incoming tide, the power plant had been almost eerie in its silence. The sudden rush of movement; the unexpected, earsplitting noise; the scream; the blaze of lights—any one of these would have been enough to make a statue jump. Certainly it was enough to startle three boys who had been nervous to begin with.

Hap was the first to go. He jumped backward, and his foot came down on nothingness. Panic-stricken, he clutched at Trip for support.

Together, they tumbled over the edge of the cube.

The fanatic heard their terrified cries and doused the lights.

It was dark again.

The trap had been sprung.

Everything was going to be all right.

In the moment of triumph the fanatic failed to notice one thing: the smallest of the three boys, the clumsiest one, had done just the opposite of what any reasonable person would expect. With the sudden flare of light he had jumped forward, tripped over his own feet, and smashed his head against the floor.

Gamma Ray Gammand was out cold.

He was alone in the dark.

But he was not in the deadly cage.

Hap and Trip were not so lucky. The tap of a fingertip against a button brought the great ten-foot-square grille smashing down to seal their Plexiglass prison.

Not that it really mattered. The walls were smooth as glass, and ten feet tall. Climbing out was impossible.

But they didn't know that yet. Stunned and aching, they lay at the bottom of the cube, too groggy even to realize that the tide was coming in. . . .

Trip Davis opened his eyes and looked up. Somewhere far above him a dim light seemed to be shining through a screen of some kind.

He shook his head and looked again.

It was the moon, shining through some sort of mesh.

His head hurt. He blinked and looked a third time. The mesh was one of the grilles that covered the tide cubes.

And he was at the bottom of the cube!

Suddenly he felt a splash of water on his arm. He looked up. An instant later it happened again. The tiniest amount of water came splashing over the cube. Trip recognized it for what it was: the leading edge of a wave. And he knew it wouldn't be long before water was pouring into the cube.

A moan next to him alerted him to the fact that he was not alone.

"Hap!" he cried, torn between delight at having someone with him, and horror that his friend was also caught in this trap. "Hap, wake up. We're in big trouble!"

Hap moaned again. Trip dropped to his knees and began to shake his companion by the shoulder.

"Huh? Whazzat? Whaddaya wan?" Hap muttered.

"Wake up!" screamed Trip, shaking him even harder. "We're in trouble!"

Another spray of water came over the edge of the cube. When it splashed onto Hap's face, his eyes blinked open.

"Where are we?"

When Trip told him, a look of horrified understanding twisted his face. He lurched to his feet, but fell back. "Help me up," he demanded. "Help me up. We've got to get out of here!"

But once on his feet, he had to admit what he had already known in his heart. The cube was escape-proof.

"There's got to be a way!" raged Trip. He began to run around the bottom of the cube, pounding against the walls as if that would somehow release them.

"Stop that!" shouted Hap. He looked around. "Where's Ray?"

Trip collapsed against one of the Plexiglas walls

and slid to the floor. A few drops of water spattered onto his head. "I don't know," he whispered. "Maybe he got away. Maybe he's dead. It won't be long before we are." He shook his head. "It's too bad you didn't bring one of those wrist things you and Wendy were working on."

"But I did!"

"Well, get busy and get us some help!"

"I don't know if this will do any good," said Hap, fiddling with the controls. "You know how well these things *don't* work."

"Do you have a better idea?" snapped Trip.

More water splashed into the cube.

"Just don't want to get your hopes up," said Hap. He began to speak into the small device. "Help! We're at the power plant."

He waited, but there was no answer.

He tapped the transmitter and tried again. "Help! We're at the power plant. Help! Power plant!"

The edge of another wave washed over the grille. There was more water this time, almost a quart. It wasn't much, but they knew it was only the beginning. The tide was moving in, and each wave would come a little farther over the edge of the box, throw in a little more water than the one before it.

It wouldn't be long before the box filled and began to sink into the deep, dark shaft.

"Help!" cried Hap desperately. He shook the little transmitter. "Help us. We're at the power plant!"

*   *   *

Wendy was just drifting off to sleep when the miniature communicator resting on her nightstand crackled into life.

"Huh?" she said, struggling to her elbows. "What's going on?"

"Help!" cried a distant voice. "Help our aunt!"

Wendy flopped her head back onto the pillow. What a stupid game. Somebody was going to hear about this tomorrow.

"Help!" cried the voice again.

"Shut up!" yelled Wendy, pushing her face into the mattress and covering her head with her pillow.

"Help our aunt!" cried the voice. "Help. Our aunt!"

But Wendy could no longer hear the desperate plea.

Her snores were drowning it out.

Hap cried out in horror as a splash of salty water from above struck the little transmitter. With the tiniest hint of a sizzle all its lights went out.

He cursed and shook the thing. It made no difference. The transmitter was dead.

And the tide was getting higher.

18

Descent into Doom

WENDY SAT BOLT UPRIGHT IN BED.

How long had she been sleeping?

She looked at her clock. Only minutes! What had woken her?

It was the words—the words pounding in her brain. She clutched her head, trying to force them out. But she kept hearing them over and over: *"Help. Our aunt."*

Where did they come from? Why wouldn't they stop swirling around in her head?

Then she remembered. She had been drifting off to sleep, and Hap had called her.

She growled. He was going to pay for that come morning. She'd teach him to fool around with something that was meant to be a tool.

What if he wasn't fooling around?

The thought leaped unbidden into her head and sent a shiver trembling down her spine.

Help. Our aunt.

What could it possibly mean?

She thought about the garbled messages they had dealt with earlier that day. The problem then had been parts of the words getting dropped off.

Help. That was simple enough. Nothing missing there.

Our aunt. What could that mean?

She threw aside the sheets. Grabbing her robe, she headed for the phone. *I hope one of the twins answers*, she thought. *I don't know how I would explain this to their father.*

Rachel Phillips was putting the finishing touches on the article she had been typing for her father when the phone ringing beside her startled her into deleting a word.

She frowned. Who could be calling at this time of night?

"Telephone!" yelled Paracelsus. "I'd get it, but you forgot to give me legs."

Wishing her twin had a somewhat less bizarre sense of humor, Rachel reached for the receiver.

"Help. Our aunt," said the voice at the other end.

"What? Who is this?"

"It's me, Wendy. Listen, help me figure out what that might mean. I think the boys are in trouble."

Rachel felt a coldness grip her heart. "What are you talking about?"

Quickly Wendy explained about the message that had come in over the wrist device.

"Do you have a lexigraphic program you can plug into your terminal?" asked Rachel.

"Great Glork! Why didn't I think of that? That's what happens when someone wakes me out of a sound sleep. Listen, you start running it, too, will you? I'm worried."

"Will do," said Rachel. "I'll call you if I figure anything out. You do the same."

"Right," said the Wonderchild. Then she clicked off.

Rachel reached for the lex program and found she was trembling. What could the strange words mean? Were the boys really in trouble? She was glad Roger had come home with her and was upstairs now, doing some of the other chores they had promised their father to complete.

She plugged the program into the terminal. More than likely the mainframe had a similar one, probably more powerful, but she had no time to search for it.

Almost instantly the screen flashed and the program title appeared: SAY THE WORD; A LEXIGRAPHIC COMPENDIUM. Seconds later the words were replaced with a colorful menu of tasks the program would perform.

Rachel selected the one she wanted, an operation

that would take part of a word and splice on beginnings and endings, then present her with the combinations that actually matched the program's massive dictionary.

. . . OUR AUNT . . . she typed in. The computer would insert beginnings on the first word, endings on the second. If she didn't find an answer that way, she would turn it around and try the reverse.

She waited for the computer to race its way through the dictionary.

Hit any key for listings said the screen.

Rachel complied, and the possibilities began to scroll past her eager eyes: FOUR AUNTS, HOUR AUNTS, SOUR AUNTS . . .

She made an angry sound. Nothing of any sense at all. Feeling desperate, she typed in a new combination.

The water was up to Trip's knees and rising faster than ever. He stood braced against the wall. Hap was standing on his shoulders, pushing against the grille.

"It's no use," he grunted. "I can't move it!"

"Try again!" shouted Trip. His shoulders were screaming for relief, but the fear of death gave him a strength he had never known he possessed. "Hit it harder!"

"I'm hitting it as hard as I can!" bellowed Hap. He smashed the palms of his hands against the grille again, but it didn't budge, not even a millimeter.

"Again!" yelled Trip, just before his knees buckled and he dropped backward. A great splash went up as Hap fell from Trip's shoulders and struck the water.

They felt the cube lurch another inch downward. The two boys huddled together miserably and looked up. The water wasn't splashing in now. It was *pouring* over the edge of their prison in a steady stream.

"How long do you figure we have?" whispered Hap.

Trip shook his head. "I don't know. It just keeps coming faster and faster...."

"Whatcha doin'?" asked Roger, wandering in to the room where Rachel was working.

"Trying to match words," said Rachel. Her voice was trembling. "I'm glad you're here."

Roger looked at his sister more closely and realized that her face was pale, her eyes wide with worry.

"What's going on?"

When Rachel had filled him in, he looked over her shoulder at the monitor. OUR... / ... AUNT were the cues she was typing in.

"Look, Rachel—I don't want to tell you what to do. But are those the kind of cues you've been typing in since you started?"

"Why?"

"Well, this program isn't all that sophisticated. All you're going to get with *aunt* are words that end with *a-u-n-t*—of which there aren't many. It doesn't do sounds. That's up to you."

"So?" Her face went white. "Oh, my God! I can't believe how much time I've wasted. What's the matter with my brain? Their message probably didn't have anything to do with anyone's *aunt*. That's just how I *heard* it from Wendy!"

Quickly she typed in a new clue.

The machine rolled up another list of possibilities: DOUR PANT, HOUR PANT, POUR PANT . . .

"You know, even now, you've got to try different readings for those things," said Roger. "That's what made it so hard to get a computer that could read aloud—the language is just so inconsistent. You never know what a set of letters is going to mean, or how—"

"Shut up and think!" snapped Rachel.

The list continued to fill the screen, now using two letter prefixes for the second word: DOUR CHANT, DOUR GRANT . . .

"I can't wait until we get to ELEPH-ANT," said Roger.

"Wait a minute!" cried Rachel. "Maybe I should be messing with *our*. How many ways can you spell that sound?"

Roger thought for a second. "There's *a-u-r*," he said, beginning to tick them off on his fingers. "And *a-u-e-r. O-u-r,* of course, but you've already used that. *O-w-e-r,* if you want to stretch the point—"

"That's it!" shrieked Rachel, before she even typed it into the computer. *"P-o-w-e-r.* Power! They're at the power plant!"

She grabbed the phone. "Where's Dad?" she asked as she punched in Wendy's number.

"Either he's still at the lab or he snuck off with some of the others for an all-night poker game."

"What's the fastest way for us to get to the power plant? Wait a minute—Wendy? This is Rachel. They're at the power plant. Meet us there!"

She hung up.

"It's not more than half a mile," said Roger. "Our best bet is probably just to run."

His twin nodded. "Then let's get going!"

"I'm scared," said Trip.

"You'd be a fool if you weren't," replied Hap.

They were standing side by side against the west wall of the cube, watching the water pour over the side. It had reached their waists and was rising fast.

Trip had a picture in his mind that he kept trying to push out. But it wouldn't go. No matter how hard he tried, all he could think of was the cube he had seen the night Dr. Standish had showed him and Ray the plant—the cube sitting at the bottom of a fifty-foot shaft.

Except there was one difference. That cube had

held nothing but water. The cube his mind kept showing him also held two dead bodies.

He smashed his head back against the wall, trying to drive out the vision.

The cube lurched downward again.

Trip knew that before long, when the weight was great enough, their journey down the shaft would begin in earnest. There would be no fits and starts then. Just a slow, steady descent into the earth, with the ocean pouring through the grille above them.

In some ways the slowness was the worst thing of all. Being hit by a truck—one sudden blinding burst of pain, and then nothing—began to seem merciful in comparison. This waiting, this slow ride to oblivion while his mind and body were free to act but helpless to do anything was driving him crazy.

Hap nudged him. "You ever think about dying before?"

"Not much. I was planning to put it off for a while."

"I think your plans got messed up, buddy. Now, me, I figured—"

Hap never did tell Trip what he figured. He cut off his words as the cube moved again—and kept moving.

The boys locked eyes. The weight had reached the critical stage. The cube was beginning its descent.

Roger and Rachel had just reached the fence that guarded the power plant when Wendy came roaring up in her parents' Volkswagen.

"Wendy!" cried Rachel. "What have you done?"

"What are you worried about?" asked the Wonderchild. "This is an emergency, isn't it?"

"I hope not," said Rachel. "I'd be much happier if it was a false alarm."

"Well, don't count on it," said Wendy. "None of them have made it home yet. I called the Swensons, but Hap's mom isn't too worried—she said he likes to sit on the beach at night. There was no sense in calling the others—Mrs. Swenson told me Trip and Ray were supposed to be spending the night with Hap. She thinks they're all just out stargazing."

"They may be," said Roger.

"So much the better," said Wendy. "Then I can have the pleasure of killing them myself for disturbing my sleep. But if you had heard that message, I don't think you'd believe that. It was a little too desperate to be a fake. Open the gate, will you?"

Roger swung it open just wide enough to let the Volkswagen pass through. He and Rachel climbed into the car. A moment later it was jouncing down the bumpy road leading to the power plant.

When they reached the front entrance they scurried out. But the door that had been open for Trip, Hap, and Ray was now securely locked.

19

The Fanatic

THE BLACK-GLOVED FIST SMASHED ONTO THE TABLE so hard that several pens and pencils flew into the air.

The transmitter had failed!

How was it possible? The scientists who had put it together were the best in the world—with the exception of those gathered for this project, of course.

The installation had been correct, of that Black Glove was certain. So what could have gone wrong?

Whatever it was, the failure was disastrous. No other transmitter could get information past the electronic shield that blanketed the island.

The trembling figure sat breathing heavily for a moment. Slowly the clenched fist began to ease open.

All right, the transmitter was malfunctioning. But

what good would anger do? The fundamental use-lessness of anger was one of the most basic elements of the training. Energy wasted on anger could be better used elsewhere.

Black Glove took three deep breaths. The anger began to dissolve. With its passing, the answer became clear, if not pleasant. It would be necessary to make one more trip into the computer, to try to discover and repair the problem.

The idea was dangerous. Every illicit foray into the great machine carried some risk of discovery. But the alternative was even worse. For the alternative was failure and disgrace, and Black Glove could not, would not, allow that to happen.

Trip had no idea how long he had been treading water. It seemed as if it might have been forever.

"You know, people pay a lot of money for a sensation like this," said Hap.

"Waiting to die?"

"No—floating in warm saltwater. If it wasn't for the sound of the water splashing over the edge, this would be a perfect sensory deprivation tank. You know, one of those places where you float in silent darkness to get in touch with your inner self."

"I'm in touch," said Trip bitterly. "My inner self is asking my outer self what it did to deserve this. In fact, it's screaming, *'How could you do this to me? How could you get me into this mess?'* I don't think I want to be in touch with my inner self any more than I have to right now. It's too mad at me."

"Suit yourself," said Hap. "But you're missing a golden opportunity." He began doing a backstroke toward the other wall of the cube.

"How can you be so calm?" screamed Trip.

"They don't call me Hap for nothing."

Trip was silent. Hap stopped swimming. "A couple of other things to consider," he said. "To begin with, maybe I'm not as calm as I look. Second, assuming I actually am, what's the point of being otherwise? Look at you. You're in a state of panic. Is it doing you any good? Is your mind clearer? Are your thoughts sharper? You know what my old man told me once? He said, 'Hap, my boy, when it's time to go, make sure you go in style.'"

"I always preferred comfort to style," said Trip.

They were silent for a little while. The cube, which had been moving slowly but steadily down the shaft for the last several minutes, seemed to be picking up speed.

The water was pouring in faster than ever.

"How long do you think we have?" asked Trip.

"Five minutes," said Hap. "Give or take a miracle."

"Hurry!" said Roger. He was bouncing from one foot to the other in his anxiety.

"I'm working as fast as I can!" snapped Rachel, who was busy taking the hinges out of the door.

Two of them already lay on the ground next to her. The third was being stubborn. "Damn!" she said suddenly.

Roger looked down and groaned. The screwdriver Rachel had been using—which they had spent several precious minutes trying to locate in Wendy's car—had just broken off at the handle.

Rachel leaned her head against the wall. "I don't know what else to do," she said.

"Let me try something," said Wendy.

"What?"

"Just stand back. I don't know if this will work; I stopped taking lessons two years ago. But I got pretty good before I quit."

Without another word, the Wonderchild let out a bloodcurdling scream and launched herself through the air.

She slammed feetfirst into the door. It fell into the building as if it had been hit by a battering ram.

"Are you all right?" asked Roger, rushing in to the office.

Wendy lay atop the broken door. "We'll worry about me later," she said, picking herself up and brushing away some splinters. "Come on, we may not have any time to waste!"

They barreled through the office, on into the power plant itself, where an amazing sound greeted their ears: two tenor voices harmonizing on "Many Brave Souls Are Asleep in the Deep."

"That's them!" cried Rachel.

"Light!" shouted Wendy. "We need some light."

The singing broke off. "Wendy! Rachel! Is that you?" The voices sounded far away.

"Where are you guys?" shouted Roger.

"We're trapped in one of the tide boxes! Be careful—there might be someone out there!"

At this warning the twins and Wendy bunched together. They looked around suspiciously, but it was too dark to see anything.

"I think they're over that way," said Roger, who had been trying to remember what Trip and Ray had told him about the power plant.

Moving together, the three began to inch their way through the darkness. Suddenly Rachel tripped over something and fell to the floor.

"Are you all right?" asked Roger.

"I'm not sure. I think I just fell over someone's body."

"Dead, or alive?" asked Wendy.

After a pause, she answered, "Alive—I think."

As if in confirmation, the still figure Rachel had fallen over began to moan.

"It's Ray!" she said. "Give me a hand, somebody."

Wendy knelt at Rachel's side and helped her bring Ray to a sitting position. Meanwhile, Roger continued to inch his way forward.

"Hurry!" cried Trip. His voice sounded desperate. "We can't last much longer!"

"Style, chum," whispered Hap. "Style."

Just as Roger made it to the edge of the floor, the lights came on above him.

"Found it!" cried Wendy triumphantly, standing next to the light switch.

Roger was too horrified by what he saw to congratulate her. He was kneeling at the edge of a ten-foot-square shaft. The rising tide was pouring over the far edge of the shaft like a waterfall. And eight or nine feet below him Trip Davis and Hap Swenson were clinging to the underside of a plastic grille that held them trapped in some kind of a box.

Less than a foot of space separated the water in the box from the grille. At the rate the surf was pouring in, that space would be filled in less than two minutes.

When it was, Hap and Trip would be gone.

His friends stared up at him, and Roger could see the look of death in their eyes.

There had to be some way to get them out of there!

He remembered Trip and Ray mentioning that Dr. Standish had spent considerable time explaining the control panel. Maybe Ray would know what to do!

"Ray!" cried Roger, running back to where his sister crouched beside the small, unconscious figure. "Ray, wake up! WAKE UP! Hap and Trip will die if you don't!"

He grabbed Ray by the shoulders and shook him.

The unconscious boy's head lolled to the side.

"Careful!" cried Rachel. "You're hurting him!"

"Hurting him?" screamed Roger. "Go take a look over there! If I can't snap him out of this fast, those two have had it!"

Rachel scurried across the floor to where Roger had stood and began to scream.

Below her, Trip and Hap were pressed almost to the grille. Their fingers were locked through the plastic grid, their bodies supported by the water. They didn't have more than nine inches of airspace left.

"Oh, jeez," said Wendy, coming up to Rachel's side.

"Water!" yelled Roger. "I need water to wake him up!"

In the back of his mind he saw the bitter irony of the situation: Tons of water were pouring into the shaft where his friends were trapped—and he couldn't wake the one person who might be able to save them because he couldn't find a way to splash some water on his face and rouse him from his stupor.

How strange if Hap and Trip should drown for lack of a cup of water!

"For God's sake, Roger, do something!" cried Trip.

The terror in his friend's voice sliced through Roger like a knife.

Wendy had returned to the control panel. But she didn't dare touch it for fear she would push the wrong button and send the boys plummeting to the bottom of the shaft. Then she spotted it: a mottled brown mug, half filled with cold coffee.

"I've got it!" she cried, running to Roger's side. Before she could reach him, she tripped. The coffee cup flew out of her hand and sailed through the air.

"No!" screamed Roger.

Even as he cried out, the cup smashed to the floor beside Ray's head. It shattered, splashing him with cold coffee.

"What?" he spluttered, pushing himself to his elbows. "What's going on?"

Roger dragged the smaller boy to his feet. "Snap out of it, Ray. You've got to save Hap and Trip."

"What are you talking about?" asked Ray, stumbling along as Roger pulled him to the control panel. "I don't understand."

"Hap and Trip are locked in one of those tide boxes. It's sinking fast. You've got to get them out."

Ray's eyes grew wide as the words finally penetrated. "My God!" he cried. The stupor fell away from him and he ran to the control panel. "Gotta remember," he muttered, scanning the buttons and levers. "Gotta remember."

"Hurry!" cried Rachel, who was kneeling at the edge of the shaft where the boys were trapped. "They're almost under."

Hap and Trip were pressed so tightly to the grille they couldn't even turn their heads to talk to each other.

"Hap, I don't want to die," whispered Trip.

"Neither do I, pal. But we're not gone yet. Looks like we may even get our miracle."

"What if we don't?"

"Then we go in style. Hold on! It's all up to—"

His last words were cut off as the water washed over them.

The box was completely submerged.

Trip wanted to scream. *Style!* he told himself. *Hold on to the last instant.*

The thought helped him keep that last precious breath.

"They're gone!" screamed Rachel.

"Ray, do something!" cried Wendy.

Ray punched a button, then another and another. The machinery began to whir, then to whine. A burning sound filled the air.

"Those are recall buttons," he said. "I don't know which shaft the guys are in, so I tried a bunch of them."

"Nothing's happening!" cried Rachel. "Roger, they're drowning!"

Looking down that shaft at the faces of her friends trapped beneath the grille was probably the worst moment of Rachel's life. It would haunt her nightmares for years to come. They were so close— she could have jumped into the shaft and reached through the grille to touch them. Yet they were too far away to save.

She couldn't stand to watch, yet she couldn't move away. To do so would have been to leave them alone. "Do something!" she cried, beating her hands against the marble floor. *Do something!*

But the tide continued to pour over the edge of the shaft, the box to sink farther and farther away.

"It's too heavy!" cried Ray. "Those arms aren't meant to lift the boxes when they're full."

Suddenly he heard a voice in the back of his head saying, *If you can't do everything, do what you can.*

"Wait a minute!" he cried. "I've got an idea!"

He scanned the board, then pushed several buttons.

"What are you doing?" demanded Wendy.

"I'm hoping those buttons work the grilles," replied Ray. "If we can't lift the boxes, maybe we can lift their lids!"

Again the whir of machinery. For a long moment nothing happened. Then a cry of triumph from Rachel lifted their hearts. "He did it! RAY DID IT!"

The three youngsters sprinted from the control panel to the edge of the floor. Slowly, slowly, five of the great grilles were rising through the water. The boxes were already so low in the shafts that the upper edge of the grilles would barely break the surface of the water. But they *were* coming up. Clinging to the center grille were Hap and Trip, their bodies thrashing with the agony of trying to hold their breath.

Suddenly the whine of the machinery grew more intense. Again, the burning smell filled the air.

The grilles stopped moving.

"What happened?" cried Wendy.

"It's too much for the motor!" cried Ray, racing back to the control panel. "I've got to cut out the other grilles!"

His finger stabbed forward like a striking snake. Four jabs, and four work lights went out.

The center grille began to rise again. As it broke the surface, Hap and Trip scrambled to its upper edge. Their heads broke through the water and they sucked in air with great, sobbing gasps.

The box was continuing to descend. With the last of their strength, they got themselves onto the upper edge of the grille. Trip's hands barely reached the edge of the floor. Roger pulled him over, then, with Rachel holding his legs, leaned over to draw Hap up.

He was still hauling his friend over the lip of the floor when someone shouted, "What in heaven's name is going on here?"

The voice, coming unexpectedly from behind them, was so startling that Roger almost dropped Hap back into the cube. Once he *was* safely up, they saw that the shout had come from Dr. Standish.

The creator of the power plant stood at the control panel. She was dressed in an old pink bathrobe, and her hair was all awry. "My God!" she cried. "What have you kids been up to?"

"No," snarled Roger, turning on her. "The question is, what have *you* been up to, Dr. Standish?"

Eyes blazing, the scientist drew herself to her full height. "Just what do you mean, young man?"

"I mean," said Roger, "that I think you had better tell us what you've been up to that's so important it justifies attempted murder."

"If you were an adult I could have you arrested for this nonsense," said Dr. Standish.

Roger stared at her coldly. He took only the briefest of pauses, then said calmly: "I only want you to tell me one thing, Dr. Standish: *When does the bomb go off?*"

"You little beasts!" screamed the scientist. She started to run.

"Grab her!" cried Roger.

But too much had happened. The gang was exhausted from the struggle to save Hap and Trip, and no one was fast enough to stop Dr. Standish as she ran past them, out along one of the small walkways between the tide shafts, and dove into the rolling surf.

A moment later her pink robe floated to the surface. But whether Dr. Standish herself had been pulled back into one of the shafts by the tide or had managed to swim out under the edge of the building, the gang had no way of knowing.

After a long silence Ray said, "How did you know she had planted a bomb, Roger?"

"I didn't. I took a guess."

"It's an old tactic of his," said Rachel.

"That's great," said Trip. "Except for one thing. From the way she reacted, there's not much doubt that she *did* plant a bomb. Only we don't know where, or when it's set to go off!"

"I think I can answer that!" said Wendy.

The others turned to her.

She was holding a battered-looking leather notebook. "I found this when I was poking around the control panel. I've only glanced at it, but it's pretty heavy. Lots of stuff about saving the world from our parents' evil computer project." She flipped to the end of it. "Lots of bomb talk, too."

"Well, how much time do we have?" asked Hap, who was sitting at the edge of the tide box, still trying to catch his breath.

"Gimme a minute. Her handwriting is the pits."

Wendy ran her finger up and down a page. "Not here," she muttered, flipping it over. "Not here. Ah—got it!"

"Well, how much time?" asked Rachel urgently.

Wendy glanced at her watch. Her face turned pale.

"If this diary is accurate, we've got less than fifteen minutes before Anza-bora blows sky high."

20

Into the Computer

THE SPRINT THE A.I. GANG MADE OUT OF THE power plant was a classic demonstration of what the human body can accomplish in an emergency. Hap and Trip, who probably should have been carried out on stretchers, were close to the front of the pack.

"Where did *this* come from?" cried Ray when they burst out of the building and came face to face with the Wendell/Watson Volkswagen.

"It belongs to my parents," said Wendy. "Hop in."

"I don't know if this is such a good idea," said Trip.

"You idiot!" cried Wendy. "The whole island is going to blow up in twelve minutes and you're worried about whether I'm old enough to drive a real car? Get in!"

They clambered in.

"Okay," said Wendy, starting the engine. "Rachel, do you remember that map of the computer center I pulled up on our terminal?"

"I remember," said Rachel as Wendy popped the little car into gear and roared up the road.

"I mean *really* remember. You're the one with the magic memory, so I'm counting on you."

"Why?" asked Roger.

"Because our friend Dr. Swimaway has planted her bomb right in the middle of the computer, and it's going to be a little like going through a maze to get to it."

They screeched to a stop behind a hedge that ran in front of the computer center.

"Nine minutes," said Ray, checking his watch. "Good luck, Roger."

The redhead sprinted up the steps. Two men were standing guard. Though they drew together to block Roger's passage, they were smiling.

"I have to get in," said Roger urgently. "It's an emergency."

"Won't it keep until morning?" asked the bigger of the guards.

"We won't be here in the morning," said Roger. "There's a bomb in there set to go off in eight minutes."

"Sure, kid. And when I go home tonight I'm

gonna spend an hour practicing ballet. Come back in the morning."

"Please," said Roger. "You've got to let me in. It's a matter of life and death for everyone on the island!"

"Yeah—we let *you* in, and *we're* dead. Amscray, kid."

"Thank you, sir," said Roger. "You've just told me everything I need to know." *And,* he added to himself as he sprinted down the steps, *given us the justification for what we're going to do next.*

Jumping into the car, he said, "Okay, Wendy. You know what to do!"

Black Glove glanced up and down the hallway. It was late, but the Project Alpha scientists frequently worked all night when they were on to something.

Not that anyone would challenge me, thought the spy, feeling slightly smug. *Still, there's no point in raising even the slightest hint of suspicion.*

Approaching the door that led into the refrigerated chamber where the computer was housed, the spy fished for the key. It was hidden beneath a supple black glove crammed in the right pocket of the lab coat.

A quick movement of the wrist and the door was open.

A last glance around showed that no one was watching.

Black Glove slipped into the heart of the computer center. But before the spy could actually reach the machine, all hell broke loose.

"Yee-hah!" cried the Wonderchild. Pressing her foot against the accelerator, she made a large circle to build up speed—then headed straight for the marble stairway that led to the main doors of the computer center.

"Hold on to your hats!" she cried as they hit the steps.

The two guards held out their rifles, then dove for the bushes as the Volkswagen bounced and rattled up the steps. Accompanied by the sound of shattering glass and twisting metal, the car exploded through the front doors of the center.

"Sorry, Mom and Dad," yelled Wendy. "It's for a good cause. Which way, Rachel?"

"Straight ahead, then left."

"Six minutes!" yelled Ray.

The Volkswagen shot down the hallway. When they reached the turn, Wendy slammed on the brakes and wrenched the wheel to the left, leaving a trail of rubber as they screeched around the corner.

"Where did you learn to drive?" yelled Hap.

"Who said I know how?" cried Wendy. "I'm making it up as I go along!"

"Take a right!" shouted Rachel.

The car squealed around the corner on two wheels, piling most of the gang in a heap against the rear passenger door.

"What if we don't make it?" asked Trip.

"Bite your tongue, Sunshine!" snapped Wendy. "You're our official optimist!"

"Down those stairs!" shouted Rachel.

"Baby, don't fail me now!" cried Wendy as she headed the Volkswagen over the edge of the stairwell.

But the little car had done its part. By the time it had bounced and bucked to the bottom of the steps, its traveling days were done.

"On foot!" cried Roger. "Rachel, lead the way!"

They piled out of the car—and straight into the arms of another security guard.

"Ray, take him out!" cried Roger.

Ray, last out of the car, circled behind the guard and launched himself onto the man's back. This startled the guard into letting go of Rachel and Trip, who went bounding down the hall.

"Dunk shot!" cried Ray, snatching off the guard's helmet and smacking him on the head with it. The guard toppled like a felled tree. Ray rode him down, then scrambled to his feet and sprinted along the hall after the others.

A metal door, painted gray, stood at the end of the hall. Above it was a flashing red light.

"Through there," said Rachel. "The computer is on the other side."

"It'll be locked," moaned Roger, pounding toward it. "It has to be."

"Two minutes!" said Ray.

A shout behind them alerted the kids to a herd of security people charging down the hall.

"They don't look happy," said Trip.

Roger reached the door first. He gave it a ferocious yank. To his astonishment, it flew open.

"Get in!" he cried. "MOVE!"

He stood at the door until the others were through. The closest guard was less than ten feet away when Roger slipped through the door and slammed it shut.

"Trip, Hap—hold it as long as you can," he ordered. "We don't need more than a minute or two."

"You don't *have* more than a minute or two," said Hap. "Go!" Shoulder to shoulder, he and Trip braced themselves against the door—less than a second before the guards began slamming themselves against the other side.

"Hold on, buddy," muttered Hap. "We made it this far. All we have to do is hold out a few minutes more."

Trip shifted his position and locked his legs. "Look at it this way, Hap. If this is it, at least we're going in style."

Then another guard slammed against the door, and there was no more time for talking.

Rachel was already heading into the center of the complex, Roger and the others close behind her.

"Look!" cried Ray.

Ahead of them was a shadowy figure. But there

203

were two many wires and crossbars for them to get a clear look at the person's face. They did catch a sense of shock and outrage. But then the mysterious figure was gone, fading into the complex like a deer into the woods.

"Forget it!" snapped Roger. "Head for the center, Rachel."

They came to a ladder. Roger scrambled up it, with the others close behind.

"That's it!" cried Rachel, pointing to an oddly wrapped package that was clearly not part of the computer.

Roger dove for it, but then hesitated once he reached it. Did he dare take a moment to study it? Or should he just yank out the wires—and pray that the bomb wasn't rigged to go off if anyone interfered with it?

He dropped to his knees beside the package. No sound, which didn't surprise him; the timer was probably electronic. His hands fluttered over the surface of the bomb, toying with the wires, then drawing back. Sweat beaded on his forehead. The fate of the island—the fate of his friends, his parents—was at his fingertips.

"Roger!" cried Rachel. *Do something!*

"Time's up!" shouted Ray.

Wincing, Roger reached out and tore a handful of wires from the bomb. For a moment, he felt as if the whole world was holding its breath.

Nothing happened.

"I think we did it," he whispered. Then, in a frenzy, he began to unwrap the bomb to make sure he really had disarmed it. After a moment he came to the timer.

"Cripes, Roger," said Wendy, looking over his shoulder. "We could have saved the car. You had five seconds to spare!"

Looking past her, Ray said, "What's *that?*"

Rachel picked up the item Ray had been pointing to. "Holy Moses," she whispered. "Get a load of this!"

Then she cried out in pain.

21

An Apology, and a Secret

THE NEXT MORNING DR. HWA SENT EACH MEMBER of the gang a message, asking them to come see him as soon as they had rested from their exertions.

It wasn't until late afternoon that the kids actually arrived at his office. Between the time they had spent being grilled by Sergeant Brody and his security team and the time they spent calming down their parents, it was nearly dawn before any of them got to bed—and even later before most of them fell asleep.

At about four-thirty they gathered in front of the building so that they could enter as a team. Wendy astonished everyone by appearing in a blouse. (It was the first top the others had seen her wear that they knew for *sure* didn't belong to her father.)

"Well," said Bridget McGrory as they entered the outer office where she held guard. "If it isn't the heroes of the day! Himself is waiting to see you. I can't exactly say that he's happy—too much gone wrong for that to be the case. But he's certainly pleased with you six."

It was hard to believe that this smiling woman was the same person who had wanted to throw them out the first time they tried to talk to Dr. Hwa.

Ms. McGrory pressed a button on her desk. A moment later Dr. Hwa appeared at his door.

"Ah, the young heroes!" he exclaimed. "Come in, come in."

As the gang followed Dr. Hwa into his office, Ray remembered the strange thing he had seen on their previous visit. Positioning himself so he could go last, he turned to peer through the crack as he closed the door behind him.

Bridget McGrory was reaching under her desk, just as she had before. Her shoulder moved slightly. Then, with a furtive glance around the room, she turned back to her keyboard.

Ray let the door slip silently into place. His brow was furrowed. *What was Bridget McGrory up to?*

Dr. Hwa led them to a conference table at the side of his room. After motioning for them to sit down, he positioned himself at the head of the table.

"To begin with," he said, "let me extend my thanks on behalf of everyone involved in Project Alpha. It would appear that you have, as they say, saved our bacon. You have my deepest gratitude.

"Second, some news. The police have captured Dr. Standish. After she swam away from you, she stole one of the island's motorboats and headed for the mainland. As I understand it, she was planning to go to her family home." He shook his head. "Such a tragedy. Dr. Standish had a great mind. There was so much she could have accomplished.

"We searched her bungalow, of course. It was filled with material from that 'Church of the Human Heart.'" His distaste showed in his expression. "What poisonous stuff! Endless twaddle about evil scientists trying to replace mankind with computers. I suppose a steady diet of that would addle anyone's brain.

"But, thanks to you six, she was stopped." He paused, then said, "I do not think you can know how important this project is to me, how much of my life, and my heart, I have invested in it. I owe you a great debt, my young friends. I do not know how I can begin to repay you."

For a moment, no one said anything. Roger and Rachel, who were sitting across from each other, locked eyes. Rachel nodded. Roger cleared his throat.

"Yes?" asked Dr. Hwa.

"Sir, the best way you could repay us is by listening to us. We came to you once to tell you about the transmitter that we found on Rachel's collar. But because it had disintegrated, you did not take us seriously."

Dr. Hwa nodded, his mouth drawing down in a frown.

"Well, it happened again last night," said Roger. "When we went into the computer to dismantle the bomb, we found something else attached to the central unit, a device that clearly did not belong there.

"The thing is, it disintegrated shortly after we discovered it, just like the first one." He nodded to his sister. "Show him."

Rachel held out her hands. An angry red line stretched across both palms. "Burn marks," she said. "I was holding the thing when it happened."

Dr. Hwa's frown grew deeper. He sat in silence for a moment, staring at his own hands. Finally he looked up. "I am going to take you into my confidence," he said quietly. "And request that you keep this information to yourselves."

Roger looked around at the others, then nodded.

Dr. Hwa nodded back, then said, "It appears that you were indeed correct about there being a spy on the island. Though we were planning to keep this quiet, for reasons relating to both morale and security, clearly there is no point in hiding it from you. The truth is, last night *two* boats were stolen from the marina. The one in which Dr. Standish fled has been recovered. The second is still missing. I have to assume that it was taken by the person who planted that transmitter."

He sighed. "I was very foolish not to believe you the first time you came to me. Though it qualifies as locking the barn door after the horse has run away, we are taking additional security measures immediately." After a pause he said, "Though I rather wish you were not aware of quite so much of what has happened here, it is almost a relief to be able to offer you the apology that I knew was due to you, but feared I would have to withhold for security reasons."

He stood, then began to circle the table, solemnly shaking hands with each member of the gang. "It is my dream that this project may save the world," he said. "You have saved it. For that, my deepest thanks, my fine young heroes."

Epilogue

BLACK GLOVE SMILED. IT HAD BEEN THE EASIEST thing in the world to steal a boat from the marina and rig it so that it headed out to sea.

Now everyone who knew there had been a spy on the island thought that the threat to security was gone.

The spy's smile faded. In one way the threat *was* gone. With the transmitter destroyed, it was going to take time to find a new way to get information to G.H.O.S.T.'s headquarters.

But that was just a matter of time. A way *would* be found.

And if those kids dared to interfere again, then whatever had to be done to stop them would be done.

Even if it meant that one or more of them must die. . . .

About the Author

BRUCE COVILLE was born in Syracuse, New York. He grew up in a rural area, around the corner from his grandparents' dairy farm. Halloween was his favorite holiday, his school's official colors were orange and black, and as a teenager he made extra money by digging graves—all of which probably helps explain why he writes the kind of books he does. He has published more than three dozen books for children, including *My Teacher Is an Alien, Goblins in the Castle, Aliens Ate My Homework* (the first title in *Bruce Coville's Alien Adventures* series); *The Dragonslayers*, the *Space Brat* books, and *The A.I. Gang* trilogy.

Bruce Coville's Alien Adventures

What happens when a tiny spaceship crashes through Rod Allbright's window and drops a crew of superpowerful aliens into the middle of his school project? Rod is drafted by Captain Grakker to help the aliens catch a dangerous interstellar criminal—in a chase that takes them all over the galaxy!

ALIENS ATE MY HOMEWORK

I LEFT MY SNEAKERS IN DIMENSION X

AND COMING SOON...

THE SEARCH FOR SNOUT

by BRUCE COVILLE

A MINSTREL® BOOK

Published by Pocket Books

1043-02